THE AMAZING WONDERTIME ADVENTUREBOX

Volume One

ANDY R. BUFORD

To Xander & Wyatt
Best Wishes
Andy R. Buford

Illustrations by
THERESA PATRICK

Cajun Son Publishing, LLC

ONE

The Failure of a Genius

A short while ago, in the not-too-distant past, a brilliant scientist works feverishly on his greatest creation. He builds and rebuilds, works and reworks, destroys and builds up again. Finally, his masterpiece is complete. Everything he learned throughout his career has brought him to this point in time. At last, he has built the most amazing thing he could ever imagine.

However, there is a slight problem with his wonderful creation. Sadly, it is a problem he cannot solve.

His creation works perfectly but, it will not work---it cannot work---for him. After many more attempts and failures, he decides to give up. He abandons his creation to a quiet spot in the woods behind his home. In his wildest dreams, he could not imagine what would happen next...

The First Adventure

TWO

A Boy, a Dog, and a Mysterious Box

Journey woke up with a sudden jolt of energy. This was the first Saturday in the new house and he wanted to go exploring in the woods behind the barn. The house wasn't exactly new, it was just new to him. It was the house his mom grew up in. During the move, she told him lots of stories about growing up there. Journey seemed to like the house just fine, but ever since he arrived on Tuesday evening, he wanted to go into the woods behind the barn.

Before the move, Journey lived in the city, and he had never actually spent any time in the woods. Now that he was living in the country, he would beg his parents to let him go into the woods every day after school.

"Not on a school night," his mother would say. "You have to do your homework, eat your dinner, and get ready for bed young man," his dad would say.

Finally, on Friday evening, when his mom was putting him to bed, she said "I know you've been anxious to go exploring in the woods behind the barn. You can do that in the morning, now try and get some sleep."

Journey woke up around 8:30 the next morning. "Wake up

Stamps. We've got a lot to do today." he exclaimed. Journey noticed two pointy ears perking up over the edge of his bed. In fact, Stamps was already awake. He was just waiting on Journey. Stamps, a Jack Russell Terrier, was Journey's dog. He was also his very best friend.

Journey got dressed and the two rushed downstairs. He was headed to the kitchen door at full speed.

"No sir," his mother shouted "you can go play after breakfast. I'm pretty sure Stamps is hungry, too."

Journey quickly filled Stamps' dog bowl and turned to see three pancakes waiting for him on a plate. He was so excited about going into the woods he completely forgot about breakfast. He thought for a second about asking to skip breakfast, but then he figured he might need the energy for his big adventure in the woods. He ate every bite and Stamps did the same.

"May I be excused?" he asked nervously.

"Where are you going in such a hurry?" she replied.

"Don't you remember? I want to go check out the woods behind the barn." he said, with his heart pounding in his chest.

"I would imagine," she said "that it might take you all day to do that. You should bring some water, and you might want to bring something to eat."

Journey couldn't believe his ears. His mother was actually going to let him stay in the woods all day! He was sure she was going to say something like "don't be gone too long" or "stay close to the house" or, even worse, "be careful." He quickly made a peanut butter and jelly sandwich, filled up his canteen, and headed out the door with Stamps trailing close behind.

"Thanks, Mom," Journey shouted as he crossed the back yard, making his way toward the barn.

"Be careful," she replied.

Journey walked along the north side of the barn, swinging a stick he picked up in the back yard. Step-by-step he walked until he rounded the back corner on the northeast side. Finally, he got his first full look at the woods. He couldn't really see them from his upstairs bedroom because the barn was so big.

He paused for a moment to take in the sight. The tree line

started about twenty-five feet behind the barn and it just seemed to go on forever from there. He remembered his dad saying something about 1000 acres but he didn't really know what that meant. He took a deep breath and walked forward.

Journey walked into the woods, which was fairly easy to do. Most of the underbrush had been cleared by his grandfather the previous spring. There were a few bushes here and there, but mostly he could walk upright between the trees. Oak trees, elm trees, maple trees and even a few trees he didn't know were all around him. He could tell these trees were very old.

He and Stamps crept steadily forward and, after they had been walking for about ten minutes, Stamps let out a tiny "woof." Journey looked down and he could see Stamps looking straight ahead, jerking his head slightly to the left and then to the right. Journey could see he was looking deeper into the woods, but he couldn't tell what Stamps saw.

"Let's go check it out, boy," Journey said. Stamps rushed forward and Journey could barely keep up. He ran behind Stamps shouting for him to slow down. They ran for almost a tenth of a mile when Stamps suddenly stopped. Journey could see that Stamps was looking at something in a clearing just ahead. "Come on, let's go see," he said. Now Journey was in the lead as Stamps followed behind.

Journey entered the clearing. Right in the middle, as if the whole clearing was made for it, was a wooden box. Journey could see it was about 5 feet wide by 3 $\frac{1}{2}$ feet deep and it was about 3 feet high. He walked around the whole thing to get a better look. He could tell it was very well made.

The box had very fancy brass hardware. It had three flat straps of brass across the top that turned into the hinges for the lid. It also had a latch in the front, but Journey decided not to open it just yet. He wanted to look at the outside a little longer. Journey noticed something odd almost immediately. Except for some dirt and grime from being outdoors, the box seemed almost brand new. He put his canteen, and the peanut butter and jelly sandwich down on a stump. Then, he took a handkerchief out of his pocket and started wiping the box to clean it up.

After he had carefully wiped down every side of the box, he decided to open it up. He turned the latch and opened the lid. He began to study the latch and he noticed it could be opened from the inside of the box as well. This meant someone could get inside the box, shut the lid, and still be able to open it. "How cool," he thought to himself.

Journey began to look around inside the box. He could see a small brass rectangle in the top right corner, but it was covered in dust. He wiped it clean and read what it said. The *Amazing Wondertime Adventurebox Serial #00001*. "What an unusual name for a box," he thought to himself.

He continued to look around inside the box. He noticed a black velvet bag with a drawstring in the bottom left corner. He gently picked it up and opened it.

There inside the bag was a small electronic tablet about 6 inches by 3.5 inches. It had one button on the bottom and a row of tiny solar cells across the top.

Journey pressed the button and the device came to life with a gentle whirring sound. Suddenly the box started playing a pre-recorded message: "Thank you for your purchase of the Amazing Wondertime Adventurebox, your gateway to excitement and adventure. If you are ready to begin your adventure, please get into the box, close the lid and press this button here." Journey looked at the screen and he could see a blue button coming into view.

He thought about his sandwich before he got inside the box. "I'll just leave it," he said to himself. He decided he should probably bring the canteen.

"Okay Stamps, are you ready to see what this is all about?" asked Journey. Stamps looked up at him and replied with a shallow "woof."

"Okay, boy. We need to get in and shut the lid," he said as he picked up Stamps and placed him inside.

He climbed into the box and closed the lid. He pressed the button. Almost immediately, Journey could tell something was happening. He looked down at Stamps and could see he was getting smaller. He looked at his hand and it too was getting smaller. Just when he was about to get scared, he heard a sound that went "*pop.*" A half a second later, he heard another popping sound. The sound itself wasn't very loud, and it seemed relaxing. He looked at himself, and then Stamps. He could tell they were both normal size again. Stamps looked for a moment like he might bark, but Journey patted him gently on the head to calm him down.

Journey carefully opened the lid of the box and started to climb out. He stood up straight to stretch then bent down to pick up Stamps. "Come on boy," he said "this adventure won't begin by itself."

The moment he set both feet onto the ground, the tablet sprang to life again. It beeped three times and the words "YOUR ADVEN- TURE STARTS NOW" showed up on the screen, and then disap- peared. "Well, Stamps, let's see what this is all about," he said as Stamps looked up at him.

* * *

THREE

The Arrival

The first thing Journey noticed when he arrived was that it wasn't quite daylight. The sun was about to come up behind him. At first, he couldn't see anything but the jungle around him. All he could hear were crickets and the sound of strange birds off in the distance. He was sure he'd never heard that sound before.

Journey got back into the box, carefully placing Stamps beside him. "I guess we'll figure out what our adventure is when the sun comes up," he said looking at Stamps as he closed the lid. "For now let's just sit here and wait."

About ten minutes later, he could hear the faint sounds of people talking and moving around. He gently opened the lid of the box a few inches and peeked out. Off in the distance, he could see several pits dug into the earth at different places.

He also saw what looked like the ruins of some ancient buildings. Over to the right, he could see about a dozen tents of different sizes. Just outside of one of the tents, three people were talking to each other.

He climbed out of the box to find himself at the edge of a forest about halfway up a hill. He thought about the box for a moment. Since it was his only way home, he figured he should probably hide it. He drug it into the forest a few feet and hid it behind a tree.

Journey looked down at Stamps and said "Let's go." As they left the woods, Journey picked up a stick and stuck it, straight up, into the ground. Then he took some large leaves from a nearby bush and stuck them on top. He stood back and thought about how it looked. He wanted it to look like some sort of flag. "That should do it," he thought. He did this to mark the location of the box so he could find it later.

"I think we should go talk to those people, boy. Does that sound good?" he asked. Stamps looked up at him and gave a gentle "huff."

The two of them started walking. The ground in front of them was covered with thick shrubs, ferns, and vines. It was easy to see where they were going, but getting there would difficult.

Journey had to walk carefully to keep from going too fast. The hill was steeper than it looked and he didn't want to fall. He kept walking until he saw a caterpillar on the ground. He stopped to look at it for a second, then continued on.

They kept walking until they reached the place where the tents were. Journey stood there a moment to look around. He could see several ancient buildings, half covered in vines. He walked around to the front of the tents, watching the people who were standing there. He could see two men and one woman.

ANDY R. BUFORD

* * *

FOUR

The Introduction

J ourney sighed as he approached the people. They looked and sounded friendly, but he was still a little nervous.

One of the men was talking to the woman, "Maybe we could get some sort of..." the man stopped talking because he noticed the woman wasn't listening. He could see on her face that she was looking at something else. He turned around, and was very surprised, to see a young boy and a dog.

"Well what, or maybe I should say who, do we have here?" asked the man.

"My name is Journey and this is my dog, Stamps. We're travelers looking for adventure." Journey said in a very confident and important sounding voice.

"Travelers...looking for adventure, you say. So tell us, Master Journey, how does someone your age get to a place like this?" the man asked.

"How I got here would be hard to explain because I'm not really sure myself. Can you please tell me your names? I would also like to know what this place is." Journey said.

"You have arrived," the man said "at an archaeological dig of an ancient city in the republic of Peru. We have been excavating here for almost a year. The current date is September 27th, 1914. Now that I've answered your questions, I must tell you, this is no place for a boy."

"Stanley!" the woman spoke up. "That's no way to treat a guest!"

"My name is Violet," she continued. "You've already met Stanley. This is Walter, and here comes Henry."

Journey noticed a third man was walking up behind them.

"It's a pleasure to meet you and your dog. I will take you to meet our boss, Professor Oldstuff, and he will decide if you can stay. Follow me." Violet said as she turned around and started walking.

"Come on, boy," Journey said in a low voice as Stamps began to follow. As they were walking, Journey suddenly realized the *Amazing Wondertime Adventurebox* had brought him *back in time*. He couldn't believe it. He started to wonder about how it was possible but, before he could think about it too long, Violet spoke up.

"Prof. Oldstuff is the lead archaeologist here. He is a very nice man. I don't think he'll mind you being here. He might even enjoy it. He loves teaching people new things," she said as they walked.

The two of them continued until they reached the very last tent. It was almost three times bigger than the other tents. Violet motioned with her hand as she said, "KNOCK, KNOCK. It's Violet, may I come in?"

"Enter," came a voice from inside the tent.

"I'll go in and tell him about you and Stamps." she said to Journey. "You two wait here until I tell you to come in."

"No problem," Journey said as he bent down to pet Stamps.

* * *

FIVE

Prof. Oldstuff

A s he stood outside the tent, Journey could hear faint whispering. He tried and tried but he couldn't make out what they were saying. Several minutes went by. It felt like he had been standing there forever.

Violet stuck her head out of the tent and said, "Professor Oldstuff will see you now."

Journey took in a deep breath and entered the tent. Violet was standing on his left and a tall, ragged gentleman was standing before him. His face was tan and wrinkled with a square jaw, but Journey could tell it was a kind face.

Prof. Oldstuff looked at him with a gentle smile and said, "Welcome to my camp, Master Journey. I hear you're an adventurer. My name is Professor Finding Oldstuff. I know, I know, it's an unusual name. My father, Professor Clement Oldstuff, was also an archaeologist and he had a strange sense of humor. So, what kind of adventure are you hoping to find here?"

"I don't know, sir," Journey replied. "Until I figure it out, could you tell me about this place?"

"I would be glad to," he said. "You are standing on an archaeological site of an ancient city. At first, we thought it belonged to the

Incas. We now think it belonged to a different people. We're not sure what they called themselves."

"Why don't you think they were Incas?" asked Journey.

"There are," Prof. Oldstuff replied, "just too many differences. The artwork, the buildings, and the writing are all completely different. We figure this city was home to about 3,000 – 5,000 people who had their own culture. I studied the Incan civilization while I was at the university, and I know this is different."

"I see," said Journey. "Can you tell me what you're working on now?"

"Well," he said, "this is a very exciting time. One of our crew found a few stone tablets with writing on them just last week. Also, we have just finished cleaning out the main building on the site. It's the tall one in the center. There is also a building on the far side of the city that was very important to these people. We don't know what is in there but it is full of traps."

"Traps?" asked Journey.

"Oh, yes," he replied. "There were trap doors, snake pits, and swinging knives, just to name a few. We've disabled all of them except one. If we could solve the mystery of the last one, it will unlock a large door on the far side of the room."

"What do you think is in there?" asked Journey.

"As a scientist," Prof. Oldstuff said, "I must deal in facts. Some of the team think it's a burial place, others think it has a treasure of some kind. I just want to get it open to find out for myself."

"WOW!" Journey exclaimed. "Can you tell me about the last trap?"

Prof. Oldstuff replied, "Well there were several traps as I said before. We built bridges across all the trap doors and snake pits. We carefully caught the swinging knives and cut each one of them down. We haven't figured out how to defeat the last trap."

"Here is a floor plan of the building that one of my team drew up," he continued. "As you can see, there are several rooms, all roughly the same size, in a row. Each room has two doors. One door is the entrance, and the other door leads to the next room. Each of these rooms contained a different trap. All the traps have been defeated except for the last one. At the end of this long hallway here is the last room, about twice as big as the others. In the center of this room is a stone pedestal about three feet high with a crystal sphere on top. The sphere is perfectly round and perfectly smooth. It must be removed in order to unlock the final door. However, when the sphere is removed, thousands of poison darts start flying out of the walls from all directions. One of my crew made it out just in time. A single dart barely scratched his arm and he became very ill. I believe if it had pierced the skin, he would have died for sure. We have tried and tried but we can't seem to figure out a way to defeat the last trap. Our supplies are running out and I'm afraid we won't be able to open it before we have to leave."

"Did you try tying a rope to the sphere so you could pull it off from a distance?" asked Journey.

"We thought of that, and we even tried it, but the sphere is so round and smooth, the rope just slipped off. After we tried it, we also realized the sphere would fall on the ground and break if we did it that way. We certainly don't want that to happen. As archaeologists, we try very hard not to break things. We need to disable the last trap and time is running out. I know you're young, but if you could find a way to help, I would be very grateful," he said.

"I'm always happy to help. I need some time to think about it, though," Journey said. "While I'm thinking, maybe you could take me on a tour of the ancient city."

"I think I can arrange that," Prof. Oldstuff said.

* * *

SIX

The Tour

P rof. Oldstuff opened the door of the tent and motioned for Journey to come out. He almost tripped on Stamps as he stepped outside. "Oh, Violet told me you had a dog. His name is Stamps, right?" he asked.

"Yes, sir," Journey replied, "and he's the best dog in the whole world. Can he come along?"

"I'm sure that will be fine," replied Prof. Oldstuff. "Follow me and I'll show you around. Over here we're digging out an area where we think they gathered for meals. Imagine a huge one room building with long stone tables. What we would call the kitchen would actually be a group of fire pits placed outside. If you look over there, you can see the dark charcoal colored dirt where they were."

"Pretty cool," Journey said.

"What was that?" asked Prof. Oldstuff.

"What do you mean?" replied Journey.

"I believe you said "pretty cool." What does that mean?" Prof. Oldstuff asked.

Journey suddenly remembered he was in the past. He realized he needed to be very careful about how he spoke. He certainly couldn't let anyone know he was from the future so he decided to say, "Where I'm from, pretty cool is a phrase people say when they like something. I liked what you were telling me about the fire pits so I said *pretty cool*."

"Pretty cool," Prof. Oldstuff said. "It is an odd phrase but it does have a nice ring to it. I'll have to remember that."

Prof. Oldstuff continued to take Journey around the city with Stamps following close behind. He was very good at explaining things so Journey could understand. He had many questions and Prof. Oldstuff was very patient with him. He seemed to enjoy telling Journey all about the history of the site.

The two of them continued the tour until they reached a large tent. They went inside and Journey could see Violet and a couple of other people sitting down at some wooden tables. Each table was covered with stacks of square pieces of stone with carvings on them. Journey knew this was some sort of writing. He remembered studying about the Egyptians and their writing, which was called hieroglyphics.

"Hello, Journey," Violet said with a smile as she looked up. "These are my helpers, Bob and Victor," she said pointing to the two men in the room.

"Do you know what these are?" she asked.

"It looks like Egyptian hieroglyphics," Journey replied.

"Well, aren't you a bright young man!" said Violet. "Well, they are hieroglyphics but they're not Egyptian. Bob and I are trying to clean them off and Victor is copying each of them onto paper. We don't know exactly what they say but we do know what some of them are about. Come see," she said as she motioned for him to follow her to another table.

Violet continued, "These tablets are about the traps and they come in pairs. We were very fortunate to find them. They were in a stone box which we thought was a coffin. Each tablet has a drawing of the trap with hieroglyphics written beneath. One tablet in each pair explains the trap, and the other tablet is the key to the solving it. We can't quite figure out what the last remaining tablet is trying to say. We think it explains how to defeat the last trap but we don't know what it means."

"Can you show me?" Journey asked.

"Sure," said Violet. "On this first tablet we can see the pedestal with the sphere on top. This last tablet is just a picture of the pedestal without the sphere. This means the sphere must be removed to open the door but, if we do that, the poison darts start flying. It really is a mystery, wrapped in a riddle."

Journey looked at the two tablets very closely. The sphere was gone on the second tablet but there was something else he noticed. He noticed it almost immediately, but he wasn't sure what it meant. The pedestal on the second tablet was clearly larger and taller than the one on the first tablet.

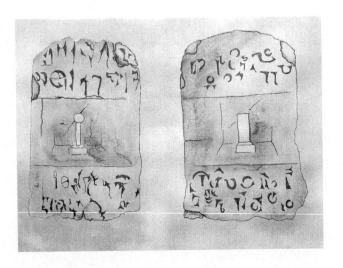

"Miss Violet," Journey said, "the pedestal on last tablet is much bigger and taller. Do you think it means something?"

"Hmm," Violet said, "I hadn't noticed that. It definitely *could* mean something, but what?"

"I need to finish the tour with the Professor, I'll think about it," Journey replied.

Journey asked the Professor if they could continue the tour and he said it would be fine. He looked around the room once again, glancing at each tablet for a short time.

"There is a waterfall near here, would you like to see it?" the Prof. asked.

"Yes," Journey exclaimed, "I would love to! How about you, Stamps? Would you like to see a waterfall?"

"Woof," Stamps replied.

Just then Violet looked up and said, "If you guys can wait just a minute, I'll go with you."

The two of them watched as she finished cleaning the tablet she was working on. She gathered a few things into a bag and slung the bag over her shoulder. "Let's go," she said.

They walked on a trail through the middle of the site and headed toward the jungle. Journey could see a path had been cleared through the trees.

Prof. Oldstuff spoke up "Some of the workers found the water-fall the first week we were here. They cleared this path so all of us could enjoy it. Sometimes we come here for lunch. It really is some-thing to see. I'm sure you're going to love it."

They continued walking and Journey began to hear a rumbling in the distance. He could tell right away it was the sound of rushing water. He had seen waterfalls on TV and in the movies, but he'd never seen one in real life. He was getting excited. He looked down at Stamps and he noticed his eyes were wide open.

"It's alright, boy," he said.

The three of them rounded a corner in the trail and suddenly the sound of the water was incredibly loud. Journey looked ahead of Prof. Oldstuff and he could see the jungle opening up in the distance. The sound was getting louder with each passing step. As they got even closer, the rumbling sound turned into a thundering sound. Journey could feel the earth shaking beneath his feet.

They finally made it the edge of the jungle and stepped out into the open. He looked over to his right and there it was. It was about seventy feet high and about two hundred feet wide. It was amazing. He just couldn't believe what he saw. It was simply magnificent.

They stood there for a while, gazing in wide-eyed wonder. After a few minutes, Prof. Oldstuff spoke up and said they should be getting back to camp. They turned around and made their way back to the trailhead.

At the edge of the jungle, Journey noticed Stamps was looking at something. He walked over to check it out. There was a turtle moving slowly toward the river. Prof. Oldstuff and Violet stopped to look at it as well. Journey looked at it closely. He had seen turtles before. This one, with the exception of how big it was, wasn't anything special.

While they were looking at it, a breeze picked up. Journey watched as a small twig fell out of a tree onto the turtle, hitting its shell. He thought about how the turtle's shell protected him from getting hurt by such things. Just then, he had an incredible thought.

"I know how we can defeat the last trap!" Journey exclaimed.

"Really?" Prof. Oldstuff asked. "Well, let's go back to my tent and talk it over. Violet, I need you to tell everyone to be in my tent in ten minutes. I'm very interested in hearing what young Master Journey has to say."

SEVEN

Building the Box

Journey waited in the tent with Prof. Oldstuff as everyone gathered for the meeting. There were more people than he expected, about twenty in all. Prof. Oldstuff stood up and began to speak.

"For those of you who don't know, we were surprised by a couple of visitors to our camp this morning. This is Journey, and this is his dog, Stamps," he said, pointing to each of them. "Journey says he has a plan to defeat the last trap and I am anxious to hear what it is. So, young man, how do we stop the poison darts?"

"We don't," Journey said. Everyone in the room, including Prof. Oldstuff, gasped out loud.

"Well, if we don't stop the darts, someone will die," said a man from the back.

"This is a waste of time," said another man. "I have a lot of work to do."

"Let me explain," Journey said. "Prof. Oldstuff and Violet took me to see the waterfall this morning. On the way back I saw a turtle heading toward the river. As I watched it, a twig fell out of a tree onto the turtle's shell. It was at that moment I figured out how to defeat the last trap."

"Go on," said Prof. Oldstuff.

Journey continued, "Miss Violet, do you remember the drawing on the last tablet, how the pedestal was bigger and taller?"

Violet replied, "Yes, I remember."

"It was bigger and taller because it wasn't the pedestal," Journey said. "It was a shelter built *around the pedestal.* Do you think one of you could build a wooden box with a lid around the pedestal and the sphere? It would need to be big enough to have a person inside as well."

A man from the back spoke up, "My name is Simon, and I'm the carpenter here. I can build whatever you want but, I think you should know, I don't have very much wood left. The person would need to be very small in order to fit inside."

Journey said, "Well, I thought of the plan so it should be me who goes inside."

Prof. Oldstuff spoke up, "I can't allow that, it is too dangerous."

"There won't be any danger at all," said Journey. "I will get inside the box and place the lid on top. After the lid is shut tight, I will lift up the sphere. This will release the poison darts. I will be protected by the box. When the darts have finished, I'll get out of the box. If the box is thick enough, and strong enough, I'll be perfectly safe."

"Amazing," Prof. Oldstuff said, "simply amazing. Never in a hundred years would I have thought of that. We were so busy trying to figure out how to stop the darts we never even considered something so simple. Are you sure you want to do this?"

"I really like helping people," Journey said. "Besides, I want to see what's behind that final door!"

Simon spoke up, "Come with me, Journey. We have a box to build."

Journey followed Simon into a large open sided tent. He could see all sorts of hand tools lying around. He was still looking around when Simon began to speak.

"I already have the measurements of the pedestal and the sphere. I need to get your measurements so I can figure out how big the box needs to be," said Simon.

He asked Journey to stand up straight against the center pole of the tent. Then, he took out a pencil and made a mark on the pole to indicate Journey's height. He measured from the pencil mark to the ground and wrote down the number. He then measured around Journey's arms and chest.

"There, that should do it," said Simon. "Your box will be finished in about an hour. You must be getting hungry. The others will be gathering for lunch soon, you should join them. They're in the tent over there," he said pointing to a nearby tent.

"Come, on Stamps," said Journey. "Let's go get something to eat!"

The two walked over to the tent and went inside. Journey could smell the food and it smelled delicious.

"Come in, come in," said Violet. "This is Tom and he's our cook.

Tom spoke up, "Today we have roasted chicken and vegetables. We also have chicken soup, if you want that instead. I get the chickens and the vegetables from a village nearby. Eat all you want, don't be shy."

Journey grabbed a plate and a fork. He took a couple of pieces of chicken and a spoonful of vegetables and put them onto his plate.

"It looks very good," he said, smiling at Tom.

Tom replied, "Thank you, I hope you enjoy it."

Journey grabbed a smaller plate. Carefully, he tore some of the chicken meat off the bone and put it on the plate for Stamps.

"Here you go, boy," he said.

Violet motioned for Journey to sit at the table with her and Prof. Oldstuff. There were two other men there but Journey didn't know their names.

"This is Alex and this is James," Violet said as Journey grabbed a chair and sat down.

Alex spoke up almost immediately, "I have to tell you, the idea with the box, truly brilliant."

"I couldn't have thought of it," James said with a smile.

"Thank you," Journey said. "Simon said it would be finished in a couple of hours. We should be able to use it this afternoon. I can't wait."

Journey finished his meal and asked Violet and Prof. Oldstuff to come with him. He wanted to see if Simon was finished with the box. The three of them made their way to Simon's tent and went inside.

"How's it coming?" Prof. Oldstuff said.

"Almost finished," Simon replied. "I need about ten more minutes."

"Well, I need Violet to show me those tablets again. Let us know when you are finished," Prof. Oldstuff said as he and Violet walked out.

Journey watched Simon work. He could tell Simon really knew what he was doing.

Just then, Simon spoke up, "I couldn't get it as tall as I wanted because I don't have enough wood. You'll be able to fit inside but you might have to bend down a little."

"I think I can do that," said Journey.

Simon put a few more finishing touches on the box and then he began to take it apart.

Journey looked a little confused by this, so Simon started to explain, "The pieces of the box fit together like a puzzle. Each piece slides into the next piece until all the pieces form a box. After the four sides are put together, just place the lid on top and you will be safe and sound. The pieces are heavy, but you can haul them on this wagon until you get to the pedestal. Why don't you practice putting this together so you'll know how to do it when you get there?"

"Good idea," Journey said as he began to gather the pieces. He struggled on his first two attempts but, on the third try, he got it. It was really easy after he figured it out.

Journey was taking the box apart for the final time when Prof. Oldstuff and Violet returned.

"So," Journey asked as he looked at the three of them, "when are we going to do this?"

"I really don't see any point in waiting," said Prof. Oldstuff. "It will be getting dark in a few hours so we'd better go now."

The Amazing Wondertime Adventurebox

EIGHT

The Final Trap

Simon grabbed the pieces and began placing them on the wagon, stacking them carefully. Journey turned around, towing the wagon behind him. Violet, Prof. Oldstuff, and Simon soon followed. Journey looked at the position of the sun in the sky and asked Prof. Oldstuff what time it was.

"2:21," he replied as he looked at his pocket watch. "The building is this way, follow me."

Journey, Simon, Violet, and Stamps all followed him until they came to the door of the building.

Just then Violet spoke up, "Journey, you don't have to do this if you don't want to. We might be able to find another way."

"Don't worry Violet, I'll be fine," he said to her. "After seeing how good Simon is at building things, I know this is going to work."

"Well, you certainly are a brave boy," she said. "Promise me you'll be careful."

Journey thought for a moment about how Violet reminded him of his mom and said, "I promise."

He turned to look at Stamps and said, "You can't come with me. Stay here with Violet until I get back." Stamps looked up at him as if to say he understood.

Journey grabbed the handle of the wagon and slowly entered the doorway. Once he was inside, he took a look around. The room was about twenty feet square with a doorway at the back. There were torches burning on the walls to provide light. He could see the light from several torches further into the building. The light was just bright enough to see everything. He could see the stone floor and, on one side of the room, several knives and ropes stacked in the corner. Those must be the knives Prof. Oldstuff talked about, he thought to himself.

He made his way to the door at the back, still taking in the space around him. The room smelled musty and it seemed very old. He tried to imagine the people who once lived here. He wondered what they were like. He wondered about their culture and what they did for fun.

He continued through each room, noticing the defeated trap in each one. He carefully walked over the bridges the crew had made over the snake pits and trap doors. He could tell they were well built, but they were still scary.

He kept going until he reached the hallway. It looked to be about forty feet long with a doorway at the end. "That's where I need to go," he thought to himself.

Journey walked through the doorway, dragging the wagon behind. He kept walking until he got to the pedestal. He stood there for a moment, looking at the crystal sphere. It had a soft glow, reflecting the light from the torches on the wall. It was very beautiful.

The pedestal was incredible. It was carved out of stone and polished smooth. The crystal sphere was perfectly round and completely clear, with no noticeable defects.

After looking at them for a little while, he decided he should get to work. He began putting the box together around the pedestal. Piece by piece, he constructed the box around himself until the only thing left to do was to place the lid on top.

Journey carefully inspected each side of the box. Gently, he closed the lid and then…*darkness.*

He hadn't thought of that. With the lid closed, it was completely dark. There was nothing he could do about it now. He was just going to have to work in the dark.

He felt around until he had both hands around the sphere. He carefully picked it up and placed it on the floor onto a cloth Prof. Oldstuff had given him. Almost immediately, he started hearing a tick, tick, tick noise.

Those must be the poison darts, he thought to himself. The

noise grew louder and louder as thousands upon thousands of poison darts flew through the air. He could hear them hitting the box and the floor and even the walls.

After a while, the noise slowed down and then stopped completely. He decided to wait a little while after the noise stopped just to be safe.

After he was certain it was all clear, he carefully opened the lid. It was heavier now. "It must be the darts," he thought to himself. He threw the lid onto the floor. He took off one side of the box so he could step out of it, allowing the other three sides to stand upright.

He turned to look at the doorway behind him…it was open. HE HAD DONE IT!

Journey almost ran inside but he stopped short. It might have some more traps, he thought. So he decided to go back and tell everyone.

He ran as fast as he could. So fast, in fact, the crew thought he was being chased by something as he left the building.

"ARE YOU ALRIGHT?" Violet screamed.

"I DID IT, I DID IT! THE FINAL DOOR IS OPEN!" he exclaimed.

"DID YOU LOOK INSIDE? WHAT DID YOU SEE?" Prof. Oldstuff asked.

Journey spoke up, "I didn't go inside. I thought there might be more traps so I decided to come back here. We can all go take a look together. Come on."

Prof. Oldstuff told Violet, Simon, and Bob to come along. "Let's all follow Master Journey and discover what he's found!" he said.

Before they set off, Journey called Stamps. "Now you can come, boy!" he said.

"Oh," Journey said, "there are thousands of darts on the floor. We might need to bring some brooms to sweep them out of the way, just to be safe."

"Thoughtful boy," said Violet.

When they saw the room with poison darts everywhere, they were simply amazed. Bob and Simon started sweeping the darts on the floor, clearing a path for them to walk. Prof. Oldstuff stopped at the place where the pedestal and the crystal sphere were. He took a good look at the pieces of the box. There were hundreds, if not thousands, of darts stuck into each of the sides and also the lid. "Incredible," he said.

"Well," Prof. Oldstuff continued, "I guess we should take a look inside. Violet, do you think it is safe?"

"Of course I can't be sure," said Violet, "but it should be. You see, we have successfully defeated all the traps on the stone tablets. So, logically, there shouldn't be any more traps."

"Makes sense," Prof. Oldstuff said. "Journey, I need you, Violet, and Bob to stay here. Simon and I will go check it out. If it is safe, we will come back to get you."

Journey couldn't help being disappointed, but he knew this was the right thing to do. They needed to be absolutely sure it was safe first.

Journey, Violet, and Bob stayed behind as Simon and Prof. Oldstuff continued on. He could hear Prof. Oldstuff and Simon talking but he couldn't make out what they were saying. After a minute or two, Simon returned.

"Follow me," he said, "and prepare to be amazed."

Bob started to rush forward but Violet caught his arm. "I think Journey should go first. We wouldn't be here without him," she said. "Journey, lead the way."

Journey walked forward, trying not to break into a run. His mind was racing and he could feel his heart pounding. He was more excited about this than he was about defeating the trap. He kept going until he reached the door, and then he went inside.

The first thing he noticed, because he couldn't help it, was gold. There were gold necklaces, gold rings, and several large, carved gold figures. He saw silver jewelry as well.

He stared at the jewelry for a little while, then took a look around the room. It was much bigger than he imagined. It was so big he had trouble trying to guess just how big it was.

"Prof. Oldstuff," Journey asked "how big do you think this room is?"

"I would imagine about twenty feet high, forty-five to fifty feet wide, and I can't be sure how long it is because I can't see the end of it from here, maybe two hundred feet or more." Prof. Oldstuff answered.

Journey tried to take it all in. He could not believe what he saw around him. In addition to the gold and silver, he saw blue and pink opals, emeralds, rubies, and some other precious gemstones he couldn't identify. He also saw several household items. There were cups, bowls, pots, and large vases. Everywhere he looked, there was some sort of treasure.

"Well, Prof. Oldstuff, you sure did strike it rich!" Journey said.

"No, young Journey," Prof. Oldstuff said with a laugh, "each of these treasures, every one, belong to the people of Peru. As archaeologists, our job is to find out all we can about the people who lived here. The knowledge we gain is our reward. We will gather as much as we can carry with us and turn all of it to the people of Peru when we get back to Lima. I will also tell them how to find this place so they can come back for the rest."

"I guess that really is the best thing to do," Journey said.

"You're a very bright and thoughtful young man, Journey. I would love to have you come to another dig site we're working on. We'll be going there as soon as we're finished in Lima. Would you like to join us?" asked Prof. Oldstuff.

"I would love to but I don't think I can. I really need to get back home," Journey said.

"I understand," said Prof. Oldstuff. "I need to get back to work. I have to write down a list of everything we'll be taking with us. Goodbye, Journey. We will miss you."

Violet heard Journey and Prof. Oldstuff talking. "You're leaving?" she asked. "Please don't go so soon!"

"I have to," Journey said. Just then, Simon came up to the two of them.

"You are the bravest boy I've ever known, except maybe for me," Simon said with a laugh. "I don't want you to leave. You know, we're about to go to another dig site."

"I came here looking for an adventure. Now that the adventure is over, I have to go back home," Journey said. "Thank you all so much for teaching me and for being so kind. Come on Stamps, we need to go back now."

Stamps perked up and began to follow Journey. Violet caught up with them just outside the large room and gave them both a hug. Journey thought he saw a tear in her eye but he didn't say anything, he just smiled and turned around. "Come on, boy," he said.

He and Stamps continued walking through each of the trap rooms until they were outside. They continued through the center of the dig site, past the other side, and up the hill where he had stored the *Amazing Wondertime Adventurebox*.

As he walked up the hill, he saw the stick with the leaves on it he had placed as a marker earlier. As he passed by the stick, he could see one corner of the box sticking out behind a tree.

"There it is, boy," he said to Stamps. "Come on, we need to get back home."

He and Stamps climbed into the box. Journey pressed the button on the bottom of the tablet. He watched as everything around him was getting smaller. "Can't quite get used to that," he said out loud.

The box went *"pop."* A few seconds later, he opened the lid. He was back in the woods behind his house. When he got back home he noticed something else. He looked at the clock in the kitchen. It was still Saturday and it was 9:32 am. That meant the *Amazing Wondertime Adventurebox* had brought him back shortly after the time he left, even though he was in Peru almost all day.

He couldn't believe the fantastic adventure he just had.

He walked into the living room where his mom was watching a cooking show on T.V.

"Back so soon?" his mother asked. "I thought you would be gone all day. Did you find anything interesting?"

"Not really, just some old box," Journey said with a grin.

NINE

Journey Gets a Visitor

"JOURNEY...JOURNEY," Journey's mom cried out. "Your Grandpa is here. He says he wants to talk to you."

Journey picked up his head so he could hear his mom. He was upstairs in his room reading a book. "I'll be right down," he replied. He continued reading until he got to the next page and carefully placed a bookmark there.

"Come on, Stamps. Let's go see Grandpa," he said as he patted his leg. Journey loved his Grandpa and he hadn't seen him since moving into the new house. He rushed downstairs to find him sitting in the living room. He was just finishing a cup of coffee.

"Come here, Journey. Let me take a look at you. I think you've grown since the last time I saw you!" Grandpa said with a grin. "Come take a walk with me. Of course, Stamps can come too," he said as he stood up.

"Sure Grandpa, I just need to get my shoes on," Journey replied. Journey put on his shoes and started to walk to the front door.

"No, Journey," Grandpa said "we need to go out the back door. I want to show you the barn."

"Mom says I can't go in the barn," he replied.

"Well, your mom told you that because I asked her to. Actually, before we go into the barn, we should probably go get the box," Grandpa said, giving Journey a wink.

"You know about the box?" Journey asked nervously.

"I should," Grandpa said, "I built it. Do you remember where you left it?"

"You built it?" asked Journey.

"Yes, Journey. I sure did," Grandpa replied.

Journey led him through the woods until they reached the clearing. When they got there, he pointed toward the *Amazing Wondertime Adventurebox* so Grandpa could see it.

Grandpa looked at the box for a moment and sighed deeply. "I guess we should probably get this back to the barn," Grandpa said as he picked up one side.

Journey grabbed the other side and they began to carry it through the woods. There were a million questions going through Journey's mind, but he decided not to ask them. No, he would just be patient and see how this turns out.

After they left the woods, Grandpa said, "Come on, we're almost to the barn. Well, that's *not exactly* true. You see, it's *not really* a barn. Oh, it used to be a barn a long time ago but it hasn't been a barn for quite a while," Grandpa said as they walked together.

They walked around to the front of the building. Journey could see two large barn doors which were locked. Over to right, there was another door. This door was normal sized and that was the one Grandpa was going to.

"We'll just put the box down right here," Grandpa said as he took a key out of his pocket and unlocked the door.

"Come inside," Grandpa said.

Journey stepped inside and saw there was another door. Grandpa placed his hand on a flat screen on the wall to the right of the door. The screen lit up and scanned Grandpa's hand. After the scan was complete, the door opened.

"Can you drag the box inside for me?" Grandpa asked.

Journey turned around and drug the box inside, walking backwards. After he was sure the box had cleared both doors, he stood up straight and turned around.

"WOW!" he exclaimed. He could not believe his eyes. This was definitely not a barn. The whole room looked like a scene from a science-fiction movie. The barn was actually a very large, one room science lab. The floor was covered in white tile. There were racks of computer equipment along the outside walls with workbenches and lab equipment taking up the center of the room. In the back, Journey could see several different sized boxes, stacked up almost to the roof, similar to the one he found in the woods.

"OK, let's talk about the box," Grandpa said. "What can you tell me about it? What do you think it is?"

Now, Journey is the kind of person who thinks before he speaks. He thought long and hard about what he wanted to say and then he spoke up. "It's a time machine made out of wood and brass, controlled by a tablet computer," Journey said with confidence.

"Journey, you are a very clever young man and I'm proud you're my grandson," said Grandpa. "However, you're answer was not completely right."

Grandpa continued. "It's *not exactly* a time machine. It does travel through time and space but you can't decide when and where it goes. You can't, for example, tell it to go to Philadelphia on July 4th, 1776. It's designed to find adventure whenever, and wherever, it can. Also, it is not made out of wood and brass. It only *looks like* wood and brass. Listen carefully, because I'm about to speak in scientific terms most boys your age won't understand. The box is a lattice of carbon fiber with an experimental battery I invented myself. The outer shell is very, very strong and cannot be broken. It is also waterproof and fireproof. It even floats."

A question came into Journey's mind and, after some thought, he decided to ask it, "Grandpa, where did it take you? I want to hear about *your* adventures."

Grandpa hung his head and let out a deep sigh. "I never got to use it, my boy," he said.

"Why not?" asked Journey.

"You see," Grandpa said, "in order for the box to work, it has to be no bigger than it is right now. According to some very specific laws of science, it would need to be as big as a five, story building to work for someone my size. The simple truth is this--I can't fit into the box. It's just too small for a grown person to use. I tried everything I could think of for almost twenty years. We both know it works, I just couldn't make it work for someone my size. So, I brought it into the woods and left it there. After a few years, I sold this place to your mom and dad and moved into town. I never thought anyone would find it and I certainly never thought anyone would use it. Although, I'm very glad you did. Now, if you want to keep using it, we need to talk about some rules. I'll write the rules down later, but for now I'm just going to tell you what they are."

"Okay, what are the rules?" Journey asked.

"Listen carefully," Grandpa said, "we need to keep it in the barn from now on. It needs to be recharged after you use it and you can't use it while it's charging. It takes a full week to recharge. If you remember to recharge it, you can have an adventure every Saturday morning. Be sure to unplug it before you use it. The charging port is in the back on the bottom right. Also, for every hour you're gone, one minute will go by here at home. For example, if you're gone for 24 hours, only 24 minutes will pass here. This next rule is very important: When you get to where you're going, you must hide the box or leave it with someone you trust. If it gets lost or stolen, you won't be able to get back home. You can use it as long as you agree to tell me about your adventures. I'll come by every Saturday afternoon so you can tell me all about them. Does that sound good?"

"It sure does!" Journey said. "I promise I'll tell you everything."

"Oh, one more thing," Grandpa added. "You must keep up your grades and listen to your parents. It would also be a good idea to start learning as much as you can about as many subjects as possible. You never know where the box will take you, and you need to be prepared. I'll help you any way I can, but you have to do most of the work yourself, understand?"

"Yes, sir," Journey said.

"Do you have any questions?" Grandpa asked.

"Yes," Journey replied. "How did you come up with the name?"

"Well, let's think about it for a moment," Grandpa said. "I think we can both agree it is *Amazing*, right?"

"It sure is," Journey said with a smile.

Grandpa continued, "I came up with the word *Wondertime* because you never really know where or when in time it will take you. It makes you *wonder* about where in *time* you are. *Adventurebox* is another word I came up with because it is a *box* that takes you on *adventures*.

"I see," said Journey. "I guess I should start telling you about where I went today. Let me tell you about an ancient city, dangerous traps, and hidden treasure."

"Wow!" Grandpa exclaimed. "I can't wait to hear more!"

TEN

The Rules

BEEP! BEEP! BEEP!

The alarm clock in Journey's room went off at precisely 7:30. He had been thinking about going on another adventure all week so he decided to get an early start.

"Wake up, boy," he said as he looked down at Stamps. "We've got a lot to do today, starting with breakfast."

Journey washed his face, got dressed, and went downstairs with Stamps following close behind. As he entered the kitchen, his mom turned around. She was at the stove making pancakes and bacon.

"Well, you're up early. I wasn't expecting you so soon. Breakfast will be ready in a minute. In the meantime, you should feed that dog," she said.

"Okay, mom," Journey replied.

"Oh," mom said "I almost forgot. Your Grandpa came by yesterday while you were at school. He said to give you this." She held out her hand towards Journey, motioning for him to grab the sealed envelope she was holding.

Journey grabbed the envelope and thanked her.

"Grandpa said not to open it until you're in the barn," she said as she finished making breakfast. "I sure wish I knew what you two were up to."

Journey ate breakfast like he was running a race.

"Slow down," his mom said. "You're going to choke."

He finished his breakfast and called out to Stamps, "Come on, boy. Let's go."

The two made it to the barn. Journey unlocked the outside door and they went inside. He closed the outside door and placed his hand on the scanner. Grandpa had entered Journey's handprint earlier in the week. The two of them walked over to the workbench next to the *Amazing Wondertime Adventurebox*.

"I wonder what's in the envelope, Stamps. Should we open it and find out?" asked Journey. Stamps looked at him and let out a gentle "woof."

Journey opened the envelope and looked at the note inside. This is what it said:

Amazing Wondertime Adventurebox
Rules and Instructions

- Unplug the *Amazing Wondertime Adventurebox* before you use it.
- Remember, for every hour you're gone, one minute will go by here at home.
- Be sure to hide the box or leave it with someone you trust. If it gets lost or stolen, you won't be able to get back home.
- You MUST leave the tablet inside the box. If it gets lost or stolen, you will not be able to get home.
- When you return, don't forget to plug in the charger.
- When you're on an adventure, try to remember as much as you can so you can tell Grandpa.
- During the week, learn as much as you can about everything you can. You should read books and research many different subjects. You never know where, or when,

the *Amazing Wondertime Adventurebox* will take you. You
need to be prepared.

Sounds simple enough, he thought to himself. He started
looking around the room for some thumbtacks. Once he found
some, he hung the rules on the wall right above the *Amazing Wondertime Adventurebox.*

"Well, Stamps," he said "I guess we should get started. I wonder
what we're going to see today. Let's find out, okay?" He picked up
Stamps and placed him inside the box and then got in himself.

He picked up the black velvet bag and opened it up. He pulled
out the tablet and pressed the button on the bottom. This time the
message was a little different.

"Welcome once again to the Amazing Wondertime Adventurebox, your gateway to excitement and adventure. Please get into the
box, close the lid, and press this button here." The blue button came
into view on the screen and Journey pressed it.

"HERE WE GO, STAMPS!" he said as everything around
them was getting smaller.

* * *

The Second Adventure

ELEVEN

The Arrival

J ourney paused for a second before opening the lid. "Rushing water," he said to himself. "I think we're on a riverbank, Stamps," he said aloud.

He opened the lid and climbed out. He started to bend down to pick up Stamps, but before he could, Stamps jumped out. "Well, someone sure is ready to get started!" he exclaimed.

The tablet came to life once again and beeped three times. "YOUR ADVENTURE STARTS NOW" glowed across the screen and then disappeared.

Journey took a good look around. The *Amazing Wondertime Adventurebox* had landed, as he had guessed, beside a river. I wonder where we are, he said to himself.

He turned around, facing away from the river, and saw a road. The road appeared to follow the river, at least for as far as he could see. He walked up the sloping riverbank until he was standing on the dirt road. He took a good look in both directions, but there was really nothing to see.

"Come on Stamps, let's hide the box in those bushes, and then we can find out where this road goes," he said. He turned back around and headed for the *Amazing Wondertime Adventurebox*. Grabbing the right side of the box, he drug it over to some bushes that were growing beside the river. After placing it carefully, he took a second look to make sure it was really hidden. "That should do it," he thought to himself.

Journey turned around and walked back up to the road. Again, he looked left and then right, but he still couldn't see anything. He decided to place a marker on a tree so he could find the *Amazing Wondertime Adventurebox* later. Carefully, he pulled a yellow ribbon out of his pocket and tied it to a tree branch. Grandpa had suggested using a ribbon as a marker and, after placing it on the branch, he realized it was a good idea.

He decided to take a look at the road itself to see what it could tell him. "Dirt road," he said to himself. "No signs, no landmarks, no clues."

"Let's sit down on the side of the road, boy," he said. "Maybe someone will come by and we can talk to them."

Journey sat down with Stamps beside him and started to throw some rocks into the river. After a few short minutes, he heard something. He looked down and realized Stamps heard it, too.

"Sounds like hoof beats," he thought to himself.

He looked down at Stamps and said, "That's a horse! Maybe it has a rider. Let's go check it out!"

He stood up and made his way back up to the road. Stamps followed closely. Looking down the road, he saw a man on a horse, and the horse was running very fast. Journey watched as the horse got closer and closer.

He tried to wave the man down, but the man yelled at him. "GET OUT OF THE WAY!" the man shouted and continued on.

He watched as the man and the horse passed them by. Almost immediately after passing Journey and Stamps, the horse let out a whine and suddenly reared up, throwing the man to the ground.

The man screamed in pain as he hit the ground. Journey quickly started running toward the man to see if he was alright.

As he got closer, he noticed the man was oddly dressed. He was wearing a blue coat with red cuffs, white pants, and a strange three pointed hat which had fallen off. "Revolutionary war uniform," Journey said to himself.

"Are you alright?" he said to the man. "I saw you fall. Are you alright?"

"My horse saw a snake in the road and reared up," said the man. "I feel so foolish. My leg is injured, it may be broken. I have a very important message for General Washington. My name is Abraham Johnson and I'm a messenger for the continental army. What is your name, young sir?"

Journey replied, "My name is Journey. I saw you fall and I came to see if I could help."

"Well, I'm afraid there's not much you can do for my leg but, if you can be trusted, I could still use your help. I have a secret message for General George Washington. I'm not worried about you reading it because it is written in code. Even so, you cannot open it. The envelope is sealed with wax. If this seal is broken, he won't accept it. If I tell you where to go, do you think you could get it to him? I'm not sure I can trust you, but I really have no choice."

Journey thought for a moment and said, "I'll be glad to help. I think I have a way to prove I can be trusted. Do you see the yellow ribbon in the tree over there?"

"Just barely," Abraham replied.

Journey continued, "I put that ribbon there as a marker for me to find later. I placed a wooden box in some bushes by the side of the river there. This box is very special to me and I can't go home without it. Like your message for General Washington, you can't open this box. It doesn't have a seal but I will know if you open it. If you promise to guard my box until I return, I'll deliver your message, and I'll bring back some soldiers to help you with your leg."

"So," Abraham said "you have to trust me and I have to trust you. Fair enough. If you help me get to your box I will guard it until you return. I won't open it, you have my word."

Journey said, "Wait right here. I need to get something." Abraham nodded as Journey walked over to the side of the road. He found a long stick with a fork in it on one end. He brought it to over to Abraham and helped him get up. "You can use this as a crutch to help you walk," he said.

"Very smart," Abraham said. "Can you get my horse? His name is Thunder. Do you know how to ride?"

"I rode a horse a couple of times at my cousin's house," Journey said. "I really liked it. By the way, this is my dog Stamps."

"Nice to meet you Stamps," Abraham said with a smile. "Thunder is a strong horse and he's very fast. You'll need to hold the reins very tight."

Journey walked along side Abraham as they walked toward the marker. He helped Abraham down the slope and walked him over to the bushes where he had placed the *Amazing Wondertime Adventurebox*.

Abraham sat down and began to speak, "There are some things you need to know before you get started. I have a lot things to tell you so listen very carefully. The message for General Washington is stored in a secret compartment on the saddle. If you look underneath the saddle, on the right side, you will find it. There are British patrols on the road but they might not be dressed in uniform. They usually travel in packs of three or four. If you see any men, either on horseback or walking, try to hide. We think they have a base nearby. We've been looking for months, but we haven't been able to find it. If they stop you, don't be scared. You're just a boy riding a horse. As young as you are, I'm sure they'll let you go."

Abraham continued, "The camp is only a few miles away. Follow this road until it splits into two roads. When you get to the fork, take the road to the right, which continues to follow the river. When you get to the camp, there will be two guards blocking the entrance. Tell them you have an important message for Mr. William Grayson. He is the aide-de-camp to General Washington and he is one of General Washington's most trusted men. When you meet him, tell him that I sent you. You must ask him this question, exactly like this: *Have you been…to the Stately Inn?* Now, repeat it back to me."

Journey looked at Abraham and said, "Have you been to the Stately Inn?"

"No," Abraham said. "There must be a pause in the middle.

Like this, *have you been…to the Stately Inn?* The pause is very important. After you ask him, he will reply: *The chicken there…is beyond compare.* Did you notice there was another pause?"

"Yes," replied Journey, "but why do I need to pause?"

"These are secret messages, for passing secret information. The pauses are put there to increase the secrecy and to fool our enemies," Abraham said. "Do you think you can do this, Journey?"

"Yes, sir," said Journey. "I know I can."

"Well then, you need to be on your way," said Abraham. "Come here, Thunder!"

Abraham watched as Thunder came closer and said, "I need you to take Journey to the camp, you be a good boy." Thunder nodded his head as if to say "yes."

Journey put one foot in the stirrup and climbed into the saddle. He looked down at Stamps and said, "Try to keep up, boy. We have a long way to go."

TWELVE

Captured

J ourney held tight to the reins as the horse powered down the road. Thunder was the perfect name for this horse, he thought to himself. Thunder was incredibly fast, but he had to be sure Stamps wouldn't be left behind. Every few minutes, he would slow the horse down so Stamps could keep up.

As he rode through the New England countryside, he was thinking about where, *and when*, he was. "No cars, no electricity, no fast food," he thought. The country was just beautiful. He could tell it was springtime. He could smell fresh wildflowers. The sun was shining and the air was crisp and cool. He thought about how nice it would be to go fishing in the river, but he knew he didn't have time for that.

He continued on down the road for a few hundred more yards and then he decided to give Thunder and Stamps a short rest. He slid off of the horse and led him down to the river. He thought it would be good to let the animals have a drink of water. Stamps followed Thunder and both of them drank quickly.

After a couple of minutes, the three of them went back up to the road, and almost ran into three men on horseback. "Oh no. I wonder if these are the men Abraham warned me about," Journey said to himself.

The first man spoke up in a thick English accent, "Well, who do we have here?"

Journey replied, "My name is Journey, sir." He thought about introducing Stamps and Thunder but he decided it wouldn't be a good idea. The three men were very rough looking. One of them had a scar across the front of his whole face. It started from the top left, went across his nose, and ended on the bottom right just above the jaw. Another one was missing a piece of his right ear. The one who spoke had no scars or missing pieces, but Journey could tell he was the roughest one of the bunch.

The man spoke up again, "Where might you be goin' on this fine day?"

"I'm just out riding, sir," he replied.

"Well, maybe you're just a boy riding a horse, but, if that's true, why does your horse have a continental soldier's saddle?" asked the man.

Journey decided not to speak because he didn't have an answer. He was caught.

"We should take him to the Colonel, he'll know what to do," said the man with the scar.

"Yeah, he'll fix you up good and proper," said the third man as he let out a wicked laugh.

"Come on, get back on your horse," said the first man as he grabbed the reins. "I've got these reins held tight, won't do you any good to try and run."

Journey remained silent as they rode along. The two men who weren't in charge kept taunting him. "Col. Mean will sure like seeing you. That's right, you're going to see Col. I.M. Mean. In case you haven't heard of him, *he is very mean*," said the one with the scar as he laughed out loud.

Journey paid close attention as they continued down the road. He watched as they got to the fork in the road. They took the left road, the opposite of the road he was supposed to take. A short distance later, one of the men got off his horse and opened a gate on the left side of the road. Journey could tell it was an old gate, and that the road behind it did not get a lot of traffic. The first man led the way until all the horses and Stamps had passed through. The man at the gate took a look around and then carefully closed the gate behind him.

The men continued to guide him down the road until Journey could see an abandoned farmhouse just up ahead. It was a large two story farmhouse which, Journey could tell, had been a nice home for someone in the past. There was a corral and a barn on the left hand side. There was also a smaller building, tucked way back in the corner of the right side of the property. He probably wouldn't have noticed it at all except he saw some men unloading some small, heavy, wooden barrels off a wagon just outside. They carefully brought each one into the building. He heard a voice from inside the building yell out, "Be careful or you'll get us all killed!"

The men stopped in front of the farmhouse and were greeted by a fourth man on the front porch. "Are you fellas so bored you're catching children now?" asked the man.

The leader of the group said "hello" and addressed the man as Capt. Twist. "Well, sir, maybe he is just a child, but his horse looks like a war horse and this is definitely a continental soldier's saddle. I wasn't sure what to do so I decided to let Col. Mean decide."

"Why didn't you blindfold him?" asked Capt. Twist. "This boy knows our location now. If we let him go, he could tell someone. Col. Mean will not be happy about this, not happy at all."

* * *

THIRTEEN

The Colonel

C ol. Ichabod Michael Mean was a completely unpleasant man. He wasn't evil, just absolutely disagreeable. He had been this way since he was a young boy. He just didn't know how to be friendly or sociable. He was not the type of man, for example, who would say "good morning" or "have a nice day." When other people would say these things to him, he would just stare at them with a blank look in his eyes. He never really learned how to be kind, or how to make polite conversation.

Eventually, this behavior landed him his current job. His official position, as he was told by his commanding officer, was patrol leader. His job was to oversee all patrols within ten miles of the farmhouse, and report any valuable information back to headquarters. After six months with no usable information he realized he was just a babysitter for a bunch of no-good soldiers who couldn't quite think for themselves. He didn't know for sure, but he was convinced most of these men were former pirates and thieves, maybe even worse. This made him even more unpleasant.

On this particular day, Col. Mean was daydreaming about being back home in England when he was suddenly interrupted. "What is it, Twist?" he shouted.

Capt. Twist spoke up, "Well, sir, it seems Baker and his crew have captured a boy, a horse, and a dog. Baker thinks the horse belongs to the Continental Army. The horse is very strong, and it has a Continental Army saddle. I hate to say it, but he could be right."

"How old is the boy?" asked Col. Mean.

"I'm not sure, sir. He looks to be about ten years old. He could be as old as twelve. There is something else you should know, and I'm afraid you won't be happy about it," said Capt. Twist.

"Well, go on! What is it?" Col. Mean asked sharply.

Capt. Twist was nervous because he knew the answer to that question was going to make Col. Mean very angry... very angry indeed. "They brought the boy here without a blindfold," he said as he hung his head and gritted his teeth.

"FOOLISHNESS! STUPIDITY!" Col. Mean shouted, as his booming voice shook the windows in his office. He took a deep breath. Capt. Twist thought he was taking a breath to calm down, but this was not the case. He was actually taking a breath so he could continue yelling. "WHAT IF THIS BOY IS INNOCENT AND WE HAVE TO LET HIM GO? HE'LL BE ABLE TO TELL EVERYONE WHERE WE ARE!"

Capt. Twist spoke in a careful, soothing tone. "I had the same thoughts as you, sir. I think maybe we should send a messenger to headquarters and explain the situation. They might have an idea about what we should do. In the meantime, we *could* talk to the boy."

"Good idea, Twist. However, don't send the messenger just yet. I want to talk to the boy first," said Col. Mean.

"He's right outside. I'll get him," said Capt. Twist as he turned to leave the office.

* * *

FOURTEEN

The Barn

Journey sighed heavily as he approached Col. Mean's office. Capt. Twist was holding tightly to the back of his shirt, guiding him as they walked. This was Journey's second adventure, but this was the first time he was truly afraid. The two continued until they reached Col. Mean's desk. Capt. Twist stood at attention and saluted.

"At ease," said Col. Mean.

"Here is the boy, sir. He says his name is Journey and that his dog is named Stamps. He won't tell me the name of his horse," Capt. Twist said.

Col. Mean paused for a moment, and then spoke up. "Captain, I would like to speak to him alone."

Capt. Twist turned and left the room as Col. Mean continued.

"My name is I. M. Mean, and I am a colonel in the service of his majesty, King George. Is there anything you would like to say to me?"

Journey thought for a second about what he should say. "My name is Journey and this is my dog, Stamps. This morning, a friend of mine asked if I would like to take his horse for a ride. I don't get to ride horses very much, so I said yes. I rode the horse for a while and decided to let him drink some water. Your men captured me shortly after that."

"The horse you were riding is a war horse. Is your friend a Continental soldier?" asked Col. Mean.

Journey replied, "With respect, sir, I don't think I should say anything else."

Col. Mean stood up and pointed his finger at Journey. He was about to start yelling again, but he stopped himself and yelled out for Capt. Twist, instead.

"CAPT. TWIST, GET IN HERE!"

The door opened and Capt. Twist walked in. "Captain, give this boy something to eat. After he's finished, bring him out to the barn. Tie him up next to the other prisoner. You should bring the horse out there, too. If the dog gives you any trouble, tie him up as well."

"Yes, sir," said Capt. Twist.

Col. Mean spoke up as the two were leaving his office, "You can spend the night in the barn. We'll see if you feel like talking in the morning."

Capt. Twist led Journey to the kitchen and gave him a plate of baked beans. Journey took a bite. He didn't like them, but he knew he had to eat. He forced himself to finish most of the plate and quietly gave Stamps what was left. After that, Capt. Twist brought the two of them outside.

Capt. Twist walked over to Thunder and grabbed his reins with his left hand. He was holding onto Journey's collar with his right hand. "We're going to the barn over there," he said as he pointed toward the barn.

Journey looked over at Stamps. Stamps was watching Capt. Twist, and it looked like he might attack him. "It's okay, boy," Journey said. "Come on." Stamps calmed down and followed Journey into the barn.

Capt. Twist handed Thunder's reins to Journey, then turned to open one of the very large barn doors. After they were all inside, he walked with Thunder toward the back. There was an empty stall in the corner and another stall next to that one with a horse already in it. Journey watched carefully as Capt. Twist tied Thunder up. He was worried about the secret compartment with the secret letter for General Washington. Thankfully, Capt. Twist left the saddle alone.

After he closed the gate to the stall, Capt. Twist led Journey over to a spot on the ground next to a man who was tied up. The man was sitting on the ground. His hands were tied behind his back, around a post. The man appeared to be asleep.

Capt. Twist made Journey sit down next to another post. Then, he put Journey's hands behind his back so he could tie them. Journey looked at the man next to him as he was being tied up. The man opened his eyes and winked at Journey. He closed his eyes again and pretended to be asleep.

"We'll see if you're ready to talk after you've spent the night in here," Capt. Twist said as he left the barn.

Once the man was sure Capt. Twist was gone, he whispered, "My name is Samson Prichard, what's yours?"

"Journey, and this is my dog Stamps," Journey replied. Journey looked at the man. He was rough looking and dirty. Journey wasn't sure if he could trust this man, so he decided to listen as the man spoke.

"They caught me three days ago," the man said. "Every day around noon, they blindfold me, then they bring me into the house to eat a plate full of nasty beans. They ask me questions while I eat, but I don't answer them. After I eat, they bring me back here and take the blindfold off."

"How did they catch you?" asked Journey.

Samson replied, "I'm a scout for the Continental Army. We heard reports the British had a secret base for patrols around here, and I was sent to find it. One of the patrols found me before I could. They captured me, covered my eyes, and then brought me back here. I know this is the place I was sent to find, but I still don't know where it is. Now, I've told you how I got here. Tell me your story. You're just a boy. Why would they capture someone as young as you?"

Journey began to speak, "I was standing on the road next to the river when I saw a man riding a horse. I tried to stop the man so I could talk to him, but he yelled "get out of the way" as he kept going. After he passed me, his horse reared up and he fell to the ground. I went to see if he was alright. He wasn't. His leg was badly damaged, maybe broken. He asked me if I could do an important favor for him, and I said I would."

Before Journey could say anything else, Samson interrupted, "The man who fell off the horse, what was his name?"

Journey still wasn't sure if he could trust this man so he replied, "I don't know if I should say."

"Well, then," said Samson, "let me answer my own question. I think his name is Abraham Johnson, and I think that's his horse, Thunder. If his name is Abraham Johnson, then I have another question for you. Hopefully this question will prove to you that I can be trusted. *Have you been...to the Stately Inn?*"

A sudden, surprised look came upon Journey's face. Samson knew the secret phrase. This meant he could be trusted. With a sigh of relief and a smile, Journey replied, *"The chicken there…is beyond compare."*

Samson replied with a laugh, "You said it exactly right, my boy. I guess old Abraham taught you good and proper. Listen, I've been trying to break free from this post for several hours. The bottom of it is loose, and I think I could break free if I could get underneath it. The problem is, I've dug down as far as I can reach. However, even if we manage to free ourselves, I don't know where we are. Escaping will be very dangerous."

Journey spoke up, "I know where we are. They didn't blindfold me and Col. Mean was *very mad* about that."

Samson's eyes opened wide and he said, "Tell me *exactly* how you got here."

Journey knelt down and began to draw in the dirt as he spoke. "After Abraham told me what I had to do, I headed down the river road. I rode for a few miles, then I decided to let Thunder and Stamps get some water. I led them both down to the river to drink. After they were finished, I went back to the road. That's where I was captured. I watched as we came to the fork in the road. Abraham told me to take the road to the right, but they chose the road to the left. We travelled down this road until we came to a road on the left with an old gate. One of the men opened the old gate and the road led us to this old farm."

"Listen, Journey, this is very important. Did you pass any other roads before you got to the one with the old gate?" asked Samson.

"No," Journey replied, "it was the first road on the left after the fork."

"Can you describe the buildings? How many are there?" asked Samson.

"Three," Journey replied. "As we came down the road, I saw the house, and the barn was on the left. In the back corner, on the right, there was a small building. Some men were unloading small wooden barrels into it. The barrels looked heavy and one man shouted from inside the building for the others to be careful."

Samson smiled and said, "I know exactly where we are. This farm used to belong to a Frenchman named Broussard. My father brought me here when I was about your age. Mr. Broussard was selling his horses and my father bought one of them. Shortly after that, Mr. Broussard left on a trip back to France to visit his family. He never returned. Some people say the ship he was sailing on sank, others say he can't come back because of the war. No one knows for sure. Now, if I could get loose from this post, I have a plan for our escape."

"You said you can't dig down any further, right?" asked Journey.

"That's right," replied Samson. "If I could, I would be able to slip the rope under the bottom of the post. Then, hopefully, I could figure out a way to get my hands untied."

Journey looked at Samson and said, "Sometimes I play a game with Stamps called *get the bug.* I point at the ground and say *get the bug,* and he digs wherever I point. Call him, tell him to *get the bug,* and show him where to dig. He can dig down until you're free."

Samson nodded his head at Journey to show he understood, then spoke, "Sounds easy. All I have to say is *get the bug?*"

Journey replied, "Yes, but you have to say it like you're excited."

"I'll try," Samson said. He looked at Stamps and, in a loud whisper, said, "STAMPS, GET THE BUG!"

Stamps perked up, but he didn't know this man. He looked at Journey as if to ask permission.

"Go on, boy. GET THE BUG!" Journey said.

Samson repeated the command and pointed at the small hole behind his back. Stamps ran over and started digging. Samson was free after just a few seconds. He turned around and looked at Stamps. "Good boy," he said.

Samson stood up and took a look around the barn. He was looking for something he could use to cut the rope. There was a workbench on one side of the barn with some tools on it. He found an old knife on the bench, but his hands were still tied behind his back, so he couldn't reach it. He bent over and moved the knife with his chin until it fell onto the floor. The knife landed on its point, sticking into the ground. Samson knelt down and grabbed it behind his back. After several minutes of trying, he finally cut through the rope. He rubbed his wrists as he stood up. "Now, let's get you free," he said, looking at Journey.

Journey couldn't help but notice how big Samson was as he walked over. He was very tall, with wide shoulders.

Samson bent down to cut Journey free, then the two of them stood up. Journey took a look around the barn. He could see the house through a small hole in the wall. "What if they come back?" he asked.

"They won't," Samson replied. "They only come once a day, for lunch – no breakfast, no supper. They fed me before you got here. Come over here, we need to plan our escape."

Journey walked over and Samson handed him a stick.

"I need you to draw me a map of the farm, exactly as you remember it," said Samson.

Journey knelt down and began to scratch at the dirt with the stick. "Here is the barn, here is the farmhouse, and the road goes out this way," he said.

"What about the little building in the back corner?" asked Samson.

"Back here," replied Journey as he drew it on the map.

Samson spoke up, "Tell me more about that building. You said some men put some small barrels in there."

"Yes, that's right," Journey said. "They looked heavy, and one man shouted at the others to be careful."

"Journey, those small barrels were powder kegs. They're filled with gunpowder. I have a plan, but it'll be very dangerous."

"I made a promise to Abraham I would get his message to Gen. Washington. I can't do that unless we escape. What's your plan?" asked Journey.

Samson said, "We need to wait until dark. I heard two of the men talking yesterday morning. One of them was complaining about standing guard at night by himself. That means there will only be one guard. We need to capture the guard and tie him up. After that, I need you to get our horses. My horse is in the stall next to Thunder. Bring the horses outside, and go over to the corral. Wait for me there. While you're doing that, I'll set fire to the building with the powder kegs. Afterwards, I'll meet you at the corral. Be ready to go."

"Why do you need to set fire to the building?" Journey asked.

"Two reasons," replied Samson. "First, if they're focused on the fire, they won't be thinking about us. Second, if I blow it up, they can't use it against my friends."

"I see," Journey said. "Aren't you afraid of getting hurt in the explosion?" he asked.

"No. We'll be halfway down the road before it blows up. The most dangerous part will be capturing the guard," replied Samson.

"How do we do that?" Journey asked.

"I really don't know," replied Samson. "I don't know where he'll be, or what he'll be doing. We should just sit down and try to relax. We still have a couple of more hours until dark. Maybe we should take a nap."

* * *

FIFTEEN

Escape

"Wake up, Journey. Wake up," Samson whispered. "We need to go, now."

Journey rubbed his eyes as he sat up. It took a second for him to remember where he was. He tried to look around the barn, but it was very dark.

"The moon is full tonight," Samson said. "This is a good thing and a bad thing. We'll be able to see where we're going, but they'll be able to see us as well. We have to be very quiet."

Samson walked over to the barn door. He lifted the latch very slowly, making sure he didn't make any noise. He stuck his head out of the door and kept it there for almost a minute.

Journey could tell he was looking at something, but he didn't know what. Just then, Samson closed the door quietly and turned to face him.

"The guard is out there, on a chair, sleeping. I watched for a while just to be sure, but he's clearly asleep," Samson said. "Help me find the rope you were tied up with."

Journey walked over to the post he was tied to earlier, and found the rope on the ground next to it. "I found it," he said.

"Good lad," Samson said as he began to tear off the bottom of his shirt. "I'll use the rope to tie his hands. While I'm doing that, you tie this piece of cloth around his mouth. We'll have to work together, and we must be quick."

"I'm scared," Journey said.

Samson put his hand on Journey's shoulder and said, "So am I, but we have to do this. Follow me, and be very quiet."

Samson walked over to the barn door, and lifted the latch for a second time. He opened the door just wide enough for the two of them to get out, and then he carefully closed it again. Stamps was trying to come too, but Journey wouldn't let him. Samson bent down low as he walked, closer and closer, to the guard. Journey did the same.

Samson carefully knelt down behind the right side of the chair to get into position as Journey stood on the left. Samson looked at Journey and, in a loud whisper, said, "NOW!"

Journey brought the cloth down over the guard's head until it was covering his mouth. He quickly tied it tight behind his head and backed away. Samson was just finished. He had tied both hands together, passing the rope through the rungs of the chair. The guard was awake now, and squirming to break free.

"That should hold him, now we need to get him out of sight," Samson said. He leaned the chair back and started to drag it over to the far side of the barn, away from the house. "I'll put him over here. They won't find him until morning," he said with a laugh.

Samson turned to face Journey and said, "Come on. I don't want to talk in front of him." Journey followed him until they were back at the barn door.

"Do you remember what you have to do?" he asked.

"Yes, I need to get our horses and wait for you at the corral," Journey replied.

"That's right," Samson said. "Go on, then, and be very quiet. Remember, wait for me at the corral. It might take a little while for me to start the fire, but just wait there."

Journey opened the barn door and went inside. Stamps was waiting for him. "Good boy," Journey said and he gave him a pat on the head. "Come on, we have to get the horses." He walked over to the stall with Samson's horse and opened the door. Samson had put a saddle on his horse while Journey was sleeping. Journey grabbed the reins and led him out of the stall. Then, he opened the gate to let Thunder out.

He gently walked the two horses over to the corral. When he got there, he slowly climbed onto Thunder's back and sat down in the saddle. He held the reins to Samson's horse as he and Stamps waited for his return.

Journey waited, and waited, and waited some more. He didn't have a watch with him, but it seemed like he had been waiting for at least twenty minutes. He looked around as he waited. The full moon was incredibly bright. He was surprised at how far he could see with just the light of the moon.

After separating from Journey, Samson went around to the back of the barn, and ran alongside the fence until he reached the small building. Earlier, when he was in the barn, he found some pine tar and a piece of flint.

Samson struggled for several minutes to light the pine tar. He just couldn't get it to catch fire. He decided to wrap a piece of his shirt around it. He tore off a little piece, and placed the pine tar inside, wrapping it into a loose ball. He struck the flint with the knife, and a spark fell onto the cloth. He watched as it burned there for a second. He struck the flint again. This time, he blew onto the cloth as the spark landed. He kept blowing until the cloth caught fire. He gathered some twigs and placed them on top. After a few minutes, he had a small fire going.

After he got the fire started, he went inside the building. It was full of powder kegs. Samson knew he couldn't just set fire to the kegs, he needed time to get away, so he came up with a plan. The entire building was made of stone, except the two front doors, which were made of wood. He realized all he needed to do was set fire to the *outside* of the doors. He knew it would take time for the fire to burn through, and this would buy enough time for their escape.

Samson carefully place three kegs just inside the doorway. Then he picked up another keg and brought it outside. He placed it on the ground and shut both of the doors. He busted open the top of the keg with the butt of his knife, and grabbed two large handfuls of the gunpowder. He rubbed the gunpowder all over the outside of the doors, then he grabbed some of the burning twigs from the fire. The gunpowder erupted into flame on the wooden doors. Samson watched for a moment, making sure the doors were on fire. Once he was certain, he ran back to meet Journey.

Journey saw the glow of the fire off in the distance. He thought for a moment about the trip ahead. A short while later, he could see Samson running through the darkness towards him.

Samson ran as fast as he could until he reached his horse. He opened the gate to the corral before climbing onto his horse. "Help me get these horses out. We need to set them free so the redcoats won't chase us," he said.

Journey followed him into the corral, and the two of them chased all the horses out. After all the horses were free, Samson spoke up, "We need to make them go with us, at least until the end of the road. Try to stay quiet."

Journey watched as Samson got behind the horses and began to guide them. He did the same as he looked down at Stamps. "Come on, boy. Let's go," he said.

As they continued on down the road, Journey looked back at the farm. He could see the fire Samson started glowing in the distance. Samson looked back, too. "It won't be long, now," he said.

Suddenly, Journey saw a bright flash, followed closely by a thundering explosion. Samson looked at him with a smile and said, "That ought to wake up old Mean and his boys. Forget about these horses, we need to go, now. HEEYAH!" he shouted as his horse started to run.

Journey was almost thrown off as Thunder surged forward. He didn't have time to say anything because Thunder started running as soon as Samson's horse did. Journey looked behind him to see Stamps trying to keep up. "Come on, Stamps," he shouted.

As they reached the end of the road, Samson jumped off of his horse to open the gate. Journey looked back at the farm one last time. He could see the outline of several men running around, looking at the fire. He could see Col. Mean yelling and pointing at the men.

Samson got back onto his horse, and they continued down the road until they came to the fork. When they got there, Samson decided to let the horses rest for a bit. "The camp is just down this road. You can deliver your message when we get there," he said.

SIXTEEN

General Washington

They continued down the road until they reached two soldiers standing guard. "Who goes there?" one of them shouted as they both raised their muskets.

"Samson Prichard and friend," Samson said as he continued forward.

"Hello, Sam. Who's your friend?" asked the man on the left.

"His name is Journey, and he has an important message for aide-de-camp William Grayson," replied Samson.

"Looks a little young to be a messenger," the man said.

"Never mind that, Thomas. Let us through," Samson said with some authority.

"Alright, alright, no need to bite my head off," the man said as he stepped aside.

Journey followed Samson through the camp until they came to a large tent. Samson got off of his horse and Journey did the same. Once he was on the ground, Journey opened the secret compartment and grabbed the letter.

Samson motioned for a young man to come over. The young man approached, and Samson told him to take care of the horses.

"Yes sir," said the young man as he grabbed the reins of the horses and led them away.

Samson look at Journey and said, "Wait here. They're expecting to see Abraham. I think I need to explain what happened before you go in."

Journey looked at him and said, "I understand. Be sure to tell them Abraham needs a doctor."

"I will," Samson said as he entered the tent.

Journey could hear Samson talking to the men inside the tent, but he couldn't make out what they were saying. After a couple of minutes, Samson said loudly, "Journey, you may come in now."

Journey entered the tent. He could see Samson standing by a man who was sitting behind a desk. He walked over to the two of them.

"Journey, this is aide-de-camp William Grayson," Samson said.

"It is nice to meet you, sir," Journey said.

The aide-de-camp spoke up, "Samson tells me you have a message from Abraham. May I see it?" he asked.

"Abraham told me to ask you a question before I give it to you," Journey said.

"Carry on. What is your question?" Mr. Grayson asked.

"Have you been...to the Stately Inn?" asked Journey.

Mr. Grayson looked at Journey and said, *"The chicken there is beyond compare."*

Journey turned to Samson with a frightened look on his face and whispered, "He said that wrong."

Samson smiled at him and asked "Why is it wrong?"

"He didn't pause, there was no pause!" Journey replied, pointing at the man.

Just then a tall man in the back of the tent began to laugh. Journey didn't notice him before, but he had been watching the whole time.

"He caught you, Will. This one's too smart for you to fool," the man said.

Mr. Grayson turned to the man and said, "Yes, sir. I believe he is. He's very clever, indeed." After he spoke, he turned back to

Journey and said, "Young man, allow me to introduce you to Gen. George Washington, Commander of the Continental Army."

The general reached out to shake Journey's hand. Journey shook his hand, but he didn't know what to say. He was face to face with George Washington. He smiled at Journey and asked if he could have the message.

"Yes, sir," replied Journey.

Gen. Washington broke the wax seal in the message and looked it over. "This message is in code," he said. "William, I need someone to decipher this," he said as Mr. Grayson walked over and grabbed the message.

"I'll see to it, straight away, sir," Mr. Grayson said.

Gen. Washington turned to Journey and asked, "Would you and your dog like something to eat?"

Journey said, "Yes sir, all I had to eat today was a plate of beans. Stamps had some beans, too. They weren't very good."

"Samson, why don't you see if you can get them some food, and yourself, too," Gen. Washington said.

Samson said, "Yes, sir," and left the tent.

"Well, Samson says you've had quite an adventure. Tell me about it," Gen. Washington said as he sat down in a chair and motioned for Journey to do the same.

Journey sat down and told him the whole story, from beginning to end. He told him about Abraham falling off his horse, about being captured by the British, and especially about the escape. He also said he was worried about Abraham, all alone, with a hurt leg.

Gen. Washington could see the concern in Journey's eyes and he spoke up, "I know Abraham personally. He's one of my toughest men. Don't you worry, old Abraham will be just fine. You and your dog can rest here tonight. In the morning, I'll detach a group of men to go get him. They'll need you to show them where he is. Can you do that for me?" he asked.

Journey replied, "I need to go back there anyway. Abraham has something that belongs to me, and I need to get it back. I think he's going to need a doctor; his leg might be broken."

"I'll see to it," Gen. Washington said. "You've been a big help to me. I don't know how to repay you."

Journey said, "You're very kind, but I don't need to be paid. The adventure was worth more than I could say."

Just then, Samson returned with the food. He had two plates, one for Journey and one for Stamps. Journey looked at the food on the plate. It was covered with a slice of beef, some vegetables, and even some apples. He was very hungry, and he ate every bite. Gen. Washington visited with him as he ate, and the two of them laughed and talked for almost an hour.

After that, Gen. Washington showed him a place to sleep. It was just some straw and a blanket on the ground, but Journey was so tired he didn't care. Stamps fell asleep next to him, and the two of them slept soundly until morning.

SEVENTEEN

The Return

S tamps heard the sounds of people moving around and decided it was time for Journey to get up, so he licked Journey's face until he was awake. Journey sat up, rubbed his eyes, and suddenly remembered where he was. He looked toward the front of the tent, and saw Samson entering in.

"Time to get up. Come get some breakfast," Samson said. "I know you must be hungry."

Journey looked at Samson and said, "I sure am. Stamps is, too." Journey got up, put his shoes on, and tried to straighten out his hair. He didn't have a comb, but he did the best he could. A short while later, he and Samson left the tent, with Stamps following close behind.

Samson led him to a group of men who were standing around a small fire. "The general wants us to get Abraham as soon as possible. We'll be taking five other men with us, four soldiers and a doctor. We have to leave right after we eat," Samson said.

"I'm glad you're coming with us," Journey said. "At least I'll know one person."

They continued walking until they reached the group of men. Samson began the introductions, "Everyone, this is Journey and

Stamps. Journey, this is Thomas Miller. He was on guard duty when we arrived last night. This is Timothy Baker, William Jenkins, Dr. Perkins, and Vernon Johnson. Vernon is Abraham's brother."

Journey shook hands with each of the men, and said "hello." He paused when he shook Vernon's hand because he looked just like his brother. Then they all sat down. Samson handed each of them a plate and a fork.

Just then, a short man walked up carrying two large skillets. "Bacon and eggs, boys," he said as he served Journey first. After each man had been served, he put the skillets on the ground for Stamps. Stamps quietly licked each skillet clean and then sat next to Journey.

Journey ate every bite and waited for the others to finish. He sat and talked with them until the meal was over. He told them about Col. Mean and how they escaped. They listened carefully to every word. When he was finished, Samson told them it was all true.

Suddenly, all the men got up and stood at attention. Journey turned around and saw Gen. Washington standing behind him. Journey stood up, dusting off his pants, and told him good morning.

"Good morning, Journey. I trust you slept well?" he asked.

"Yes, sir," Journey replied. "Very well."

"If you gentlemen are done eating, you need to be on your way," Gen. Washington said. "Journey, I am truly grateful for your help. The message you brought me was very important. One of my spies wrote it, and it contains information about where the British army will be next week. Is there anything I can do to repay you?"

"No, sir," Journey replied. "This has been a terrific adventure for me, it was all very exciting."

"Well, if you ever need a favor, I owe you one," Gen. Washington. "Thank you so much for your help. Goodbye, Journey. Take care, young man. I wouldn't want you to get captured again."

Journey smiled and said "you're welcome" as he shook his hand. Then Samson led all the men over to the horses. Journey recognized Thunder right away and climbed into the saddle. Stamps looked up at him and barked a tiny bark. "Calm down, boy," Journey said. "We won't be going so fast this time."

Each man mounted his horse. Then they set off to find Abraham. After they left the camp, Dr. Perkins spoke up. "I'm worried about Col. Mean and his boys. What if they find us? What if they start chasing us?" he asked nervously.

Samson replied before Journey could, "Col. Mean and his boys might see us, but they won't be chasing us. We let all their horses go when we escaped. The last time I saw their horses, they were running away from the explosion and the fire I set."

All the men, including Dr. Perkins, thought this was very funny. Timothy Baker laughed so hard he almost fell off his horse. They continued riding, laughing, and telling stories as they went.

After a while, Journey started to recognize where he was. He looked at Samson and said, "I tied a yellow ribbon in a tree around here somewhere. That's where we'll find him."

They went a little further, and then, Journey saw the ribbon up ahead. He gave Thunder a gentle kick and said, "HEEYAH!" Thunder leapt forward, increasing his speed with each step. When they were close to the ribbon, Journey pulled back on the reins, bringing Thunder to a gentle stop.

Suddenly, a voice came through the trees, "Is that you, Journey?"

"It's me Abraham, and I brought some friends of yours," Journey replied as he tied Thunder to a tree.

Each of the men walked down to the riverbank, with Dr. Perkins in the lead. Abraham was stretched out on the ground, rubbing his sore leg. The *Amazing Wondertime Adventurebox* was still hidden in the bushes, exactly where he left it.

The doctor looked carefully at Abraham's leg. "I don't think it's broken," he said. "Probably just a fracture, but we need to make a brace for your leg so you can travel. Some of you men find me some branches and some rope."

Abraham looked at Journey and whispered, "I didn't look inside your box, I promise."

"I believe you," Journey said. "I'm sorry I couldn't get here sooner. I was captured yesterday. They captured Samson, too. We escaped last night.

72

"What about the message? Did they find the message?" asked Abraham.

"No, they didn't. I brought it to Gen. Washington myself. He was very happy," Journey replied.

"That's good news. I'm glad I trusted you, Journey. You're a fine young man," Abraham said.

"I'm glad to see you. I was worried about you, out here by yourself, with a hurt leg," Journey said.

Abraham laughed and said, "I've had worse nights."

By this time, the men and Dr. Perkins were finished with the brace on Abraham's leg. "Come on men, let's help him up," Dr. Perkins said as they carefully helped him get back to the road. They walked with him until he reached his horse. Two of them stood by as he climbed into the saddle.

Samson and Abraham were talking quietly as everyone was getting ready to leave. Samson turned to Journey and said, "If it weren't for you and your dog, I'd still be tied up in that old barn. I don't know how to thank you."

"Me, neither," Abraham said. "What are you going to do now?"

Journey looked at both of them and said, "I need to get back home."

"You just be careful. I don't want you to get captured again," Samson said.

Journey said, "I will. You be careful, too."

He watched as the men rode off into the distance. He thought for a moment about his adventure, and then decided it really was time to get back home.

"Come on, boy," he said to Stamps. The two of them made their way back to the *Amazing Wondertime Adventurebox* and climbed inside. Journey pushed the button on the tablet and watched as the sides of the box were closing in. A brief moment later, they were back in the barn behind his house.

"This is a whole lot better than the last barn I was in," he thought to himself.

* * *

EIGHTEEN

Grandpa's Visit

Journey was very tired when he got back home, so he decided to take a short nap. He tried going to sleep for over an hour, but he just couldn't. He was wondering if he should keep using the *Amazing Wondertime Adventurebox* because getting captured really frightened him. He wasn't sure if he wanted to go on any more adventures, and he was worried it might upset his grandpa.

Journey went into the barn around twelve-thirty. He decided not to bring Stamps because he wanted some time alone to think about what he should do. He really did enjoy his first adventure down in Peru, but the second adventure really shook him up. He also didn't want to disappoint his grandpa.

He was still thinking about it when Grandpa walked in just before one o'clock. Grandpa knew right away something was wrong. He looked at Journey and said, "Why so glum, chum?"

Journey looked up at his Grandpa and his eyes began to water. "Grandpa, I don't know if I want to have any more adventures."

Grandpa could see Journey was clearly very upset, so he gave him a hug and said, "Hey, hey, it's alright. Tell me what's wrong."

They both sat down and Journey told him the whole fantastic tale about his latest adventure. When he got to the part about getting captured, his hands started shaking. He kept talking until he reached the end and then he said, "I really was very scared. If Samson hadn't been there, I would have been terrified. I'm just not sure I want to do this anymore. Please don't be upset with me."

Grandpa hugged him again and said, "Listen, I would never make you do anything you don't want to do, but I don't think you should make up your mind this minute. You should take the time to think about it a while, because you're very emotional right now. Take it from an old timer like me, emotional decisions are usually wrong. Do you understand what I'm saying?"

"I think so," Journey replied.

Grandpa looked at Journey and said, "Ever since I found out you were using my invention, I've been working on some upgrades for it. I won't tell you what the upgrades are, but I will tell you I have an idea for another upgrade that should put your mind at ease. I should be finished with them by the middle of the week. I can come by Wednesday after you get home from school and show them to you. Let me show you the upgrades, then you can make up your mind, alright? After you see the improvements I've made, whatever you decide will be fine with me. Fair enough?"

"That sounds good," Journey replied.

"Until then, tell me more about George Washington! What was he like?" Grandpa asked.

The two of them continued to laugh and talk until Grandpa had to leave.

NINETEEN

Upgrades

Grandpa arrived around four o'clock Wednesday afternoon. Journey and Stamps were already waiting for him in the barn. Grandpa sat down at one of the workbenches and said, "The upgrades are ready, we just need to test them out."

Journey watched as Grandpa took a laptop out of a large black bag. He turned the laptop on and waited for it to boot up. Then he took a small cable out of his pocket. He plugged one end of the cable into his laptop, then he plugged the other end into a small port on the back of the *Amazing Wondertime Adventurebox*.

"This upgrade," Grandpa said, "will change your clothes while the *AWA* is taking you to your destination. This will help you blend in with the people around you, and it will also provide you with the right clothes for the environment, like a coat, for example." Grandpa tapped a few keys on his laptop and Journey watched as the upgrade finished.

Journey thought about how Grandpa called the *Amazing Wondertime Adventurebox* the *AWA*. That sure is easier to say, he said to himself. He also thought about what kind of clothes the *AWA* could make.

Grandpa reached into his pocket and pulled out a small,

wooden box. He placed it onto the workbench and opened it up. The box contained two items; a small, metallic device with a flat red button in the middle, and something that looked like a dog collar.

"This," Grandpa said, "is the upgrade I thought of when you told me how scared you were. I want you to have a good time on these adventures, but I don't want you to be scared. This device is a panic button. Take it with you when you travel and keep it in your pocket. Also, make sure Stamps is wearing his collar. If you get scared, press this button. Once you press it, you and Stamps will be transported back inside the *AWA* and it will immediately take you back home. I think we should test it to see if it works. Help me take the box into the back yard."

The two of them took the box outside and then Grandpa said, "Now, take Stamps up to your room and press the button. If this works, you will be transported into the *AWA*, and then the *AWA* will bring you back into the barn."

Journey told Stamps to follow along as the two of them went upstairs. When he got there, he looked outside the window, waved at Grandpa, and pressed the red button. In the blink of an eye, he and Stamps were inside the *AWA*, and then they were back inside the barn. Fantastic, Journey thought to himself as he and Stamps got out of the box.

Grandpa came in from the backyard and said, "Wonderful. It worked faster than I expected. Now tell me, will the panic button keep you from being afraid?"

"I think so," Journey said. "But what if Stamps and I aren't together? I couldn't leave him behind."

"That's a very good question," replied Grandpa. "It works based on where the two of you are *in time*. You could be a thousand miles apart and it won't matter. As long as the two of you are in the same time period, it will bring both of you back to the *AWA*, and then safely back home.

Journey looked at Grandpa and said, "I just thought of something."

Grandpa said, "What's that?"

"I could use the panic button if someone steals the box," replied Journey.

"Why yes, I suppose you could," Grandpa said. "I think you should still hide it, though."

"Yes, sir," Journey said. "I will."

Journey looked at Grandpa and, with a huge grin, said, "Well, I guess I'll be going on another adventure this Saturday. Thank you, Grandpa. Thank you so much."

"You're welcome," Grandpa said. "Remember, even with the panic button, you still need to be careful. It won't keep you from getting hurt, understand?"

"Yes, sir," Journey replied. He was so excited about not having to give up using the *AWA*, he began to daydream about all the adventures he'd be having. He wondered if he would meet any more famous people, and he wondered where the *AWA* would take him next.

* * *

The Third Adventure

TWENTY

Getting Ready

The following Saturday morning, Journey and Stamps woke up at the same time. Journey got dressed and remembered to put the panic button in his pocket. Stamps was already wearing the collar because Journey thought it looked good, so he never took it off. Both of them ate breakfast, and then the two of them went over to the barn. They climbed inside the *AWA* and Journey closed the lid. He pressed the button and, as usual, everything started to get smaller. He heard a sound that went "pop" and, in an instant, they were both normal sized again.

Stamps looked for a moment like he might bark but Journey patted him gently on the head to calm him down. "Quiet, boy. I'm trying to listen," he said. He could hear waves crashing… and seagulls. "I think we're on a beach," he said as Stamps looked up.

Journey opened the lid. To his amazement, he and Stamps had, in fact, landed on a beach. He stood up straight to stretch, then he bent down to pick up Stamps and noticed something. His clothes had changed. He was still wearing a shirt and some long pants, but they looked *older,* like they were made a long time ago. The shirt had large buttons and the pants did too. No zipper, just buttons. "Come on boy," he said, "this adventure won't begin by itself."

The moment he set both feet on the ground, the tablet sprang to life again. It beeped three times and the words "YOUR ADVEN-TURE STARTS NOW" showed up on the screen and then disappeared. "Well, Stamps, let's see what we're doing today," he said as Stamps looked up at him.

TWENTY-ONE

The Island

Journey was looking at the waves crashing on the beach when he heard a noise behind him.

"Hello!"

He turned and saw three men standing at the edge of the jungle.

"Hello!" one of the men repeated as they walked towards Journey. "My name is Tsoak (pronounced SO-ack). I am a member of the Gonnado tribe and I welcome you to our island. Please come with us to meet our king. We will cook a large feast and you will be our honored guest." Tsoak explained.

"Nice to meet you, Tsoak," Journey replied, "my name is Journey and this is my dog, Stamps. We would love to meet your king, but I can't leave this box on the beach."

"Very nice to meet you Journey. We can carry your box back with us," Tsoak replied, motioning to the other two men to go and get it.

"Okay, then. Let's go," Journey said as he patted his leg to get Stamps to follow along.

On the way to the Gonnado village, Tsoak told Journey about the Gonnado tribe. They had been living on the island for hundreds of years. He told Journey they were great fishermen. He told Journey the Gonnado's were a very happy and peaceful people.

"I can't wait for you to meet our king," Tsoak said. "He's a very good king and he loves to have visitors. Sadly, we don't get visitors very often."

They kept walking for a few more minutes and then Journey began to hear the sounds of the village up ahead. He could hear children laughing and someone was playing music. They walked a little further and Journey noticed a clearing up ahead. When they entered the clearing, he saw the villagers walking around, going through their daily routines. He could see the huts which were very nice and expertly built. And then one of the villagers, a woman, noticed him walking with Tsoak and the other two men.

"Oooohhh! We have company! We have company!" she shouted.

"Yes, we have company," Tsoak said very seriously. "Quick, run and tell the king we have a visitor and his name is Journey. He also brought a dog named Stamps."

"Oh the king will be very happy," said the woman as she started to run.

Suddenly, more of the villagers noticed what was going on and they all rushed to meet the new visitor. Journey was a little nervous at first because they were all crowding around him. Tsoak noticed Journey was becoming a little worried so he decided to speak up.

"Friends," Tsoak shouted, "please give our guest some room. Everyone will get a chance to meet him tonight at the feast."

The crowd obeyed and backed away except for one little boy. Journey could tell he was about three years old. The boy just stood there for a few seconds. He looked at Tsoak cautiously and then bravely walked up to Journey and shook his hand. Before Tsoak could say anything, the boy turned around and ran off.

"His name is David. He is the youngest in the village and he is a very brave warrior," Tsoak said with a wink and a grin. "Come, we should go and meet the king."

* * *

TWENTY-TWO

The King

_____

Journey followed Tsoak to the far side of the village, with Stamps staying behind to play with the children. Off in the distance he could see a large hut. It was the biggest building in the village; he figured it must belong to the king. Tsoak walked right up to the front door and gave it a knock.

"I need to see the king; we have a visitor," he said to the man at the door.

The man opened the door wide and said, "I heard we had a visitor. Lela came by. She told us about Journey and Stamps. Welcome, Journey! The king will be very excited to meet you."

Journey followed Tsoak into the hut. He could see the hut was clean and very well kept. There were treasures and trinkets placed on shelves, and some very nice rugs. On the left side of the room, he could see a bookshelf with about 200 books on it. There were also several books spread out across the floor.

"Come in, come in!" said a loud booming voice from across the room. "I am Whacha Gonnado and I am king of the Gonnado tribe," the king announced.

"I'm very pleased to meet you, sir. My name is Journey. I have travelled here with my dog, Stamps. He's outside, playing with the children. We are both very happy to be here," Journey said.

"Tonight, we will have a feast in your honor, but until then, let us visit. I'm eager to find out more about you and your dog. I would also like to know how such a young boy could travel so far," said the king.

Journey told the king about how the *AWA* takes him on adventures, but he made the king promise to keep it a secret. The king was amazed to hear about the *AWA* and he promised not to tell anyone.

"I noticed you have a large collection of books. Do you like to read?" he asked the king.

"Those books are my most precious treasures. Sadly, no one in the village, including myself, knows how to read," the king said, hanging his head. "Perhaps *you* could teach us?" he asked.

"I would love to, but I won't be here that long," Journey said.

"Oh well. Maybe someday we will have a visitor who can help us," said the king. The king sighed and sat down in his chair.

"I'm sure of it," Journey said as he sat down in the chair next to the king.

Just then a woman came into the hut and whispered into the king's ear. "Fine, just fine," the king said to the woman.

"Come, they tell me the food is ready. It is time for us to celebrate your arrival," the king announced. "I can't wait to meet your dog."

TWENTY-THREE

The Feast

J ourney got up and followed the king to a large open area in the
middle of the village. He hadn't notice it on the way in
because Tsoak had led him along the outer edge. Up ahead, he
could see a large fire with meat and vegetables cooking on an iron
grate. At first, all he could smell was the smoke, but then, he smelled
the food. Everything smelled delicious.

"Come and sit next to me as the guest of honor. You may bring
your dog as well," the king said.

Journey sat on the cushion next to the king and made himself
comfortable. At that very moment, music began to play. A group of
young girls came in from the right and started to dance while a
group of young men came in from the left. The men were twirling
fire batons and throwing them into the air. Journey had never seen
anything like this. It was an amazing show.

After the dancers and baton twirlers were finished, a girl, around
fifteen years old, stayed behind and began to sing. She was very
beautiful, with long, thick hair, and she had a lovely voice. She sang
a slow, sad song and everyone in the village was stone quiet. After
the slow song, the musicians started playing another tune that was

more upbeat and happy. The girl started singing this song and the whole village joined in. Journey could tell that these were good people.

Journey was handed a plate which was overflowing with food. He could see meat, vegetables, fruit and bread. He was also handed a glass of juice. "Thank you," he said graciously.

While he was eating, he and the king continued to visit. "I feel really bad that I can't help you learn to read. Is there anything else I could help you with?" Journey asked.

"I don't think so. We're all very happy and content," said the king.

Just then a young boy, about five years old, whispered something into the king's ear. The king looked at him and nodded his head.

"Perhaps there is something you could do to help us," said the king. "You told me you travel in your magic box, and that it finds adventures for you to have. Is that right?"

Journey nodded in agreement, "Yes, that's right," he said to the king.

I just might have an adventure for you, if you're interested. I must warn you, though, it could be very dangerous. You will have to be very brave."

Journey thought about this for a minute. He knew if it got too dangerous, he still had the panic button. He also knew, whatever this was, he had to help. "Can you tell me what it is you need?" Journey asked.

The king sat up straight and began to speak, "On the full moon of every month, we try to have a party. We have dancing, singing, and a great feast, much like the one we're having now. I say we try to have a party because, after about an hour, we hear this terrible shrieking sound from deep in the jungle. The sound is so terrifying it scares the little children. We end up having to stop the festivities and go home. This has been happening for a long time. I am surprised it hasn't happened tonight. The villagers call it the *thing with no name* and they are terribly frightened of it. If you could help, I would be in your debt," the king explained.

Journey decided he should find out more before agreeing to help. "What does this thing look like?" he asked.

One man spoke up and said, "It is a foul creature, ten feet tall."

Another man said, "Ten feet tall? Don't you mean twenty feet tall?"

Then a woman said, "That thing is thirty feet tall as sure as I am standing here."

Journey said, "Please, tell me more."

One young man stood up and said the thing had razor sharp claws. Another said it had long fangs. Another man said that it *didn't* have fangs, but it *did* have sharp teeth that could bite a full grown tree in half.

Journey could tell by the way they were talking that none of these people had actually seen the creature. The king leaned in and asked "Will you help us? Tsoak can show you where it lives but he will only take you as far as the river."

Journey thought for a second and said "I'm gonna do it!"

"GONNADO!" the whole village shouted together.

"When will you go?" the king questioned.

"Right after we eat," Journey replied, "but I will need someone to look after my dog."

Just then, the girl who sang earlier spoke up and said, "My name is Tika. He can come home with me." Journey looked at her and said, "Will you watch him until I get back? He won't be any trouble."

"I sure will," she said with a gentle smile.

"Stamps," Journey said, "you go with this young lady and stay with her until I get back." Stamps let out a gentle "woof" to show he understood.

Journey ate until he was full and told Tsoak he was ready. Tsoak led him to the supply hut to gather some things for the trip. He handed Journey a sword and a shield. He also handed him a helmet, but it was too big for him to wear, so he put it down. Tsoak put the sword into a scabbard and put it around Journey's waist. "You will need to carry this torch in order to see. The sword and shield will be there if you need to defend yourself." Tsoak explained as he lit the torch. He also lit a torch for himself and grabbed a rope. "Come, we have a long way to travel."

Tsoak walked out of the hut and began heading west into the jungle. "This trip will take all night. Try to keep up and watch your step," Tsoak said as he picked up the pace.

* * *

TWENTY-FOUR

The Thing With No Name

Journey continued to follow Tsoak throughout the night into the deepest part of the jungle. The two of them hardly talked as they made their way through the dense plant life. He was beginning to wonder how much further they had to go when, suddenly, he could hear the sound of running water up ahead.

"We're almost to the river. I will help you get across, but the king said I can't go. Do you understand?" asked Tsoak.

"I understand," Journey said as he felt the panic button in his pocket.,

They got to the river at dawn and realized it was light enough to see. Tsoak tied the rope around Journey's waist. "The river is slow here and the water is not deep. You should be able to cross but, if you fall, I can pull you back and we can try again. When you get to the other side, tie the rope to that rock over there so you can use it on the way back. There is a trail that will lead you to where the creature lives. You will find a field with tall grass at the end of the trail. There is a cave on the far side of the field. The creature lives in the cave. I will wait here for you until midday, then I must go back."

Journey nodded his head to show he understood and carefully began to cross the river. He was very tired, but the cold river water quickly woke him up. The current was slow and he was able to cross the river in no time. He tied the rope to the rock and started off down the trail.

He had a million thoughts running through his head. Why did he agree to do this? How big was this thing? What would he say? What should he do? He mustered up all his courage and continued walking until he reached the clearing. Once again, he remembered the panic button and touched his pocket to make sure it was still there. Whatever was going to happen was about to happen right now.

Journey slowly crept about halfway across the field until he could see the cave. He was about to shout out to the creature when he noticed something. The sun was coming up and, in just a few moments, it would be shining right into the cave. Journey figured this would give him an advantage, so he decided to wait patiently.

He waited and watched as the sunlight lit up the entire entrance of the cave. Journey could see the creature sleeping, but something was wrong. The creature was very large, but certainly not thirty feet. It had big hands, but no claws. He also could not see any fangs.

Journey stood about fifteen feet from the mouth of the cave and, bravely, he shouted, "Get up you thing with no name. Get up and face me!"

Journey steadied himself as the creature began to move.

The thing sat up, rubbed its eyes, and began to yawn. He stood up and stretched. He covered his eyes from the glare of the sun and said, "Steve."

Journey was about to shout at the creature again but then he realized that it had spoken.

"What?" he asked.

"My name," said the creature "is Steve. Which is a perfectly fine name if you must know. What makes you think I have no name, and what are you doing here, anyway?"

"I'm sorry, the villagers told me you didn't have a name. I came here to tell you to quit scaring them. Every time they try to have a party, you yell and scream, then they get scared and go home," Journey said.

"I AM NOT YELLING...I AM NOT SCREAMING!" Steve said loudly.

Journey stepped back and said cautiously, "What is it, then?"

"I AM...crying. I can hear them, you see. I can hear them laughing...and playing music...and singing. I can smell the food cooking. I heard it just last night but I just went to bed early. It makes me sad. I'm so incredibly lonely here in my cave. All I have are my books to keep me company," Steve said.

As Steve talked, Journey crept slowly toward the mouth of the cave. When he got to the cave opening he realized Steve wasn't a creature at all. He was just a man. He was a big man, over six feet tall, but he was *just a man.*

Then Journey noticed something else. There were books everywhere. "I won't hurt you, Steve," Journey said as he put down his sword and shield. "I would like to know more about the books. How did you get so many?"

"Please come in and have a seat, I won't bite. Come in and I'll tell you my story," said Steve. Journey walked into the cave and sat down on a large, flat rock.

Steve sat down as well and began to speak, "Well now, you're just a boy. You waited until the sun was in my eyes to give you the advantage. That was very clever, very clever indeed. Well, let me begin. Many years ago, I was a sailor on a merchant ship. My ship came to this island to gather supplies and wait out a storm. The next morning, I was asked to look for some fresh water. I headed out into the jungle to do just that. During my search, I fell down and hit my head, which knocked me out. I woke up a few hours later and my ship was gone. I've been here, all alone, ever since. Anyway, you asked about the books. About seven years ago there was a terrible storm in the middle of the night. The next morning, I took a walk down to the beach. There were dozens of large boxes all over. Each one of them was stamped PBJ Library. I carried the boxes, one by one, back here to the cave. Each box was filled with books. I carefully opened each one, placing the books in different piles. They sat there for several months until one day I picked one up. I started to look at the words. My mother had taught me a few words when I was a boy so I knew some of them. I studied the words very carefully, trying to imagine the sounds they would make. Slowly, over several months, I taught myself how to read."

"I've never seen so many books outside of a library. Do you know how many there are?" Journey asked.

"7,267, and I've read them all, some of them twice. I have books on science, engineering, mathematics, and biology. I have funny books and sad books. I have love stories and adventure stories. You name it, I probably have a book about it," Steve replied.

Journey was amazed by the number, and variety, of books Steve had. He remembered King Whacha Gonnado had some books and that no one in the village could read. Just then, Journey had a thought. A wonderful, crazy kind of thought. He wasn't sure if it would work but he had to try.

"Steve, do you think you could teach someone else to read?" Journey asked.

"I suppose I could," Steve replied, "but who would I teach?"

"When I was at the village, the king showed me his collection of books. When I asked him about his books, the king told me that none of the villagers know how to read. Maybe, if you could teach them they would invite you to their parties. If you follow me back, I will tell them about you and your books. I will tell them you are friendly, and you mean no harm. I will also tell them you know how to read and that you will be happy to teach them," Journey said.

"Do you really think that would work?" Steve asked.

"I don't know for sure, but it wouldn't hurt to try. Come on, we have to hurry back to the river. One of the villagers is waiting for me there, but he will only wait until noon," Journey said anxiously.

Steve said "I am a very fast runner, please get on my back. I can have us there in no time."

Journey got onto Steve's back and held on tight. He could not believe how fast they were moving. They got to the river just as Tsoak was walking away.

Journey called out, "TSOAK! STOP!"

Tsoak turned around. Suddenly his eyes filled with fear. The thing with no name had taken Journey and was coming for him as well.

Journey yelled again, "TSOAK, PLEASE STOP!" He got down from Steve's back and shouted once again, "IT'S OKAY! THIS IS STEVE AND HE IS A FRIEND! WAIT FOR US THERE, WE ARE COMING ACROSS."

Tsoak couldn't believe it, the thing was friendly and his name was Steve! He decided to wait and he watched as Steve carried Journey across the river.

After they crossed, Journey shook Tsoak's hand and said, "Thank you for waiting. I would like you to meet Steve. Steve, this is Tsoak. Tsoak, this is Steve."

Both of them looked a little nervous, but they nodded and smiled at one another. Steve stretched out his hand for Tsoak to shake. Tsoak nervously did the same. They shook hands and smiled once more.

Journey motioned for the three of them to sit down. He explained to Tsoak about Steve knowing how to read. He also told him Steve would teach the whole village if he could just go to the parties. Tsoak told Journey the king would be very happy to hear this.

"Tsoak, I can find my way back to the village. You go back and tell the king the good news. Tell the village the thing with no name is actually called Steve. Tell them he is a friend and he will teach them to read. Tell them we will be there soon and to prepare another feast," Journey said.

"I sure will. Everyone will be so surprised!" Tsoak said as he started running.

"Come on, Steve. We will walk a little slower to give the villagers time to hear the news and prepare. When we get there, you can meet my dog. His name is Stamps," Journey said.

Journey and Steve continued to walk and talk until they reached the edge of the village. Steve seemed a little nervous, but Journey told him everything would be fine. Steve slowly walked into the center of the village. Everyone, including the king, was just looking at him. No one spoke up. Just then, David, the little boy who shook Journey's hand earlier, ran up to Steve. Steve bent down to get a closer look. David stretched out his hand and Steve gently shook it. Everyone in the village began to laugh.

Tika brought Stamps back to Journey and said he was a good dog. She told Journey they played for several hours the night before.

The king invited Steve to the party. He showed Steve his books and Steve was very happy to see them. The two of them became the best of friends. At the feast, Steve shook hands with every single villager, some of them twice! He also met Stamps and played ball with him.

Journey knew Steve would never be lonely again. He also knew it was time for him to get back home. He said goodbye to everyone, especially the king, Tsoak, and Steve. Two of the villagers brought the *AWA* back to him. He put Stamps inside and said goodbye once more as he closed the lid. He pressed the button on the bottom of the tablet and, in an instant, was back in the barn.

TWENTY-FIVE

Grandpa's Visit

Journey met Grandpa in the barn later that afternoon. The two of them sat together and Journey told him all about his latest adventure.

"This one was pretty easy," he said as Grandpa listened carefully. I didn't have to solve any traps, or escape from being captured. Still, I was glad to help the Gonnado tribe and Steve. I think it was a good thing for me to bring them together."

"You're a good boy, Journey," Grandpa said as he gave Journey a hug. "Now, tell me again about how you waited for the sun to come up. That was very clever."

* * *

About the Author

Andy R. Buford is an information technology professional with over two decades of experience in the field. In his spare time, he loves to write children's books and technical self-help books.

He currently lives in Longville, LA with his wife, Aimee. Together, they have two children, Tabitha and Paul. They also have a cat that acts like a dog.